THE DUKE'S BRIDE

ERICA RIDLEY

Dukes, Actually

The Duke's Bride

The Duke's Embrace

The Duke's Desire

Dawn With a Duke

One Night With a Duke

Ten Days With a Duke

Forever Your Duke

***Gothic Love Stories*:**

Too Wicked to Kiss

Too Sinful to Deny

Too Tempting to Resist

Too Wanton to Wed

***Magic & Mayhem*:**

Kissed by Magic

Must Love Magic

Smitten by Magic

The *Wicked Dukes Club*:

One Night for Seduction by Erica Ridley

One Night of Surrender by Darcy Burke

One Night of Passion by Erica Ridley

One Night of Scandal by Darcy Burke

One Night to Remember by Erica Ridley

One Night of Temptation by Darcy Burke

Welcome to Christmas!

Our picturesque village is nestled around Marlowe Castle, high atop the gorgeous mountain we call home. Cressmouth is best known for our year-round Yuletide cheer. Here, we're family.

The legend of our twelve dukes? Absolutely true! But perhaps not always in the way one might expect...

~

CHAPTER 1

September 1814
Cressmouth, England
Across the park from Marlowe Castle

"This way, if you please."

Jack Skeffington—genteel landowner, eligible widower, and exhausted father of indefatigable twins—led his business associate through a hidden panel behind his office escritoire to a secret room lined with shelves of mementos from various exploits of days long past.

Redmire gave a knowing smile. "Walls have ears, do they?"

At first glance, one would not guess Redmire to be a pirate-for-hire. Of the two men, Jack was the one with a jagged scar down one cheek and the tip of one ear missing, giving his left side a somewhat elfish appearance. A piratical elf with a terrifying dimple. Who had ignored his wounds and won the fight, thank you very much.

In contrast, Redmire practically looked like a country vicar.

Jack lit several candles and threw himself into the closer of two plush leather chairs. "Who cares what the walls hear? My staff keeps secrets very well. It's my offspring who cannot grant a moment's clemency."

"You're hiding from... ten-year-olds?" Redmire asked politely.

"I'm shielding innocent children from the mundane drudgery of balancing smuggling routes with cargo manifests in order to refine transportation timetables." Jack flapped a hand at the box in Redmire's arms. "Is there brandy in there or not?"

"Brandy *and* champagne." Redmire set his pistol on the tea table next to the empty wine glasses and knelt upon the Axminster carpet to pry open the wooden box. He handed two lovingly packed bottles to Jack, then settled in the chair opposite.

Jack grinned. "I was right?"

"You're always right... when it comes to

people's taste for illegal wine." Redmire crossed his boots atop the wooden box. "Although it required a wee bit of finesse. I reminded the distributors that our soldiers and the Prussians drank champagne from this very vineyard to celebrate Bonaparte's defeat in April."

"Did you do the bit about taxes?"

"I did." Redmire's smile widened, revealing a mouthful of crooked teeth. "'Bypassing French export taxes'—and English import tax, but who's counting?—'means each sip is like defeating Boney anew.'"

"Worked every time?"

"*Every* time." Redmire motioned to the bottles in Jack's lap. "Don't be churlish. Open it."

"With pleasure." Jack placed the brandy on the floor and set about uncorking the bottle of Madame Clicquot's legendary champagne. He filled Redmire's glass first, then his own.

Closing his eyes in pleasure, Jack lifted his glass to his nose and inhaled. The piquant effervescence masked some of the subtle aroma, but the slightly mineral, fruity taste transported him at once to the Reims vineyards in the east of France, where the grapes for Veuve Clicquot went from tiny buds in the fields to racks of bottles on the riddling table where sediment was removed from the necks before shipping.

"Are you playing your game?" Redmire asked drolly.

"It's not a game. It's a... daydream," Jack admitted. "And, yes. I was imagining what it would be like to own and manage a vineyard like Clicquot's."

"Rather than financing certain distribution channels from afar? A lot of work, I'd wager. Stick with your little village of perpetual Christmastide." Redmire pantomimed a chill. "I glimpsed a dozen parked sleighs as I crested the mountain."

"Likely queued for annual maintenance at the le Duc smithy. Autumn comes early in Cressmouth, and so does winter. We'll have snow before you know it, and those sleighs will be the only hacks worth hiring."

Redmire shuddered. "I prefer the sea, if you please. Don't you miss the days when we used to—"

The hidden panel leading to Jack's office swung open, and a four-and-a-half foot tall replica of Jack himself burst through the door. Overlong dark brown hair, thickly lashed dark brown eyes, but high spots of color on his flushed cheeks instead of the mark of a sword.

"Frederick," said Jack with well-practiced patience, "I am in the midst of an important meeting."

Sometimes, saying *Frederick* in a stern tone of voice was enough to stem the tide.

Not today.

"I'm trying to trundle hoops with the lads," Frederick burst out in wounded glory, "but Annie insists on trundling hers right where we're racing ours, and she's ruining everything!"

Redmire leaned over, one hand covering his mouth. "Last I recall, your Annie was a hoyden more than capable of keeping her own with the neighborhood lads."

"That's no doubt the problem," Jack murmured back. "I bet she's winning."

"It's not fair!" Frederick's arms stiffened with indignation. "We're twins and she's taller and I told her to go and play with flowers but she said she's tired of flowers and I said to go and trundle hoops with her own friends and she said my friends were her friends and I said they weren't, that's why they're called *my* friends, and she said, 'Piffle, one needn't be friends with a lad to best him at hoops,' and then she—"

"Frederick," Jack interrupted, keeping his tone calm and modulated. "I promise I will speak to your sister. *After* my meeting. In the meantime, you must try to get along, even if that means letting her trundle hoops with you."

"But," Frederick spluttered, "but she doesn't *listen* to me!"

"Women never do," Redmire said sagely. "Now, go on lad, your papa's busy paying a pirate for smuggled goods."

"*Aargh.*" Frederick spun on muddy heels and stalked out the door.

"What is wrong with you?" Jack hissed at Redmire in exasperation. "You can't *say* that."

"What does he think we're doing?"

"Backgammon?"

Redmire arched his brows at the tea table. "With pistols?"

"I don't know how to play backgammon!"

"It's lovely," Redmire said. "You should try it."

Jack leaned to one side to peer out the open doorway. "Frederick, the secret panel?"

A pregnant pause, then stomping boots, a huff of martyrdom, and a slam of the door.

"Thank you, my son." Jack refilled the wine glasses. "Where were we?"

"Champagne. Our orders have tripled, and we need new routes." Redmire dug a map out of the wooden box and shook out the folds. "This was our best harbor, but the government now has a blockade. What do you think if we…"

Jack might dream of owning a small vineyard one day, but his true forte lay in logistics. He compared Redmire's map to several of his own, cross-checking each with coded journals containing details of each port, route, and shipment. Before they'd even drunk half the bubbly Veuve Clicquot, new passages had been routed, along with contingency plans in case additional blockades sprung up without warning.

"Magnificent." Redmire tucked the new maps into his greatcoat and handed Jack a scrap of parchment. "This is your slice after commissions are deducted. The deposits will be made across the usual channels."

Jack's chest lightened and he let out a slow whistle. "With this, I'll finally be able to—"

The secret door bounced open and a coltish virago burst into the room.

"See this?" Annie jabbed a finger at three ragged rapeseed flowers caught in her tangled brown hair. "A moment ago, *this* was a crown of yellow flowers."

"It looks like a bird's nest," Redmire said helpfully. "An ugly one."

"Exactly." Annie turned her scowl toward Jack and waited expectantly.

He sighed. "Do you need me to do the crown?"

"No." She stomped over to his chair, spun around, and dropped to her knees. "I need you to do my hair."

Redmire choked on his champagne. "Never say you're too miserly to hire a maid."

"We have scores of maids," Annie informed him loftily. "But Papa can do it faster."

Jack placed his glass of champagne on the tea table next to Redmire's pistol and plucked the wilted flowers from Annie's hair. When she'd left the house an hour ago, her unruly brown curls had been corralled into a thick plait. Now, she sported... well, a bird's nest. Redmire was right.

With nimble fingers, Jack loosened the tangles and set about putting things to rights. "It's not kind of you to tease your brother."

"He's not vexed because I teased him," Annie grumbled. "He's vexed because I beat him at his own game."

"Everybody knows that. You don't have to prove it all the time." Jack reached the end of the plait and looped it back to her nape to secure it with a ribbon. "Besides, is it even fun anymore if you win *every* time?"

"Yes," Annie and Redmire answered in unison.

Jack patted her shoulder to let her know the plait was done. "I'm not asking you to lose on purpose. I'm asking you to give him some time to be with his friends once in a while. You have many interests. I'm sure you can find something else to entertain you for an hour or two."

She glanced at the tea tray. "Can I have a pistol?"

"No," Jack said firmly.

Annie sighed. "Not until I'm fifteen?"

"Knives at fifteen," he reminded her. "Pistols when I say so, which might be never."

She scowled. "I can do what I want when I'm one-and-twenty."

"God help us all." He motioned toward the door. "Find something to do besides tormenting your brother. We've almost finished our meeting. Afterward, Redmire will teach us all how to play backgammon."

Annie brightened. "Maybe I'll best Fred at that, too."

She skipped from the room, closing the hidden panel on her way out.

Redmire swung a disbelieving glance toward Jack. "What is the point of a secret door if everyone knows about it?"

"The government doesn't know about it," he pointed out. "It's still a valid hiding spot."

"For what?" Redmire asked. "You don't keep contraband in here. You keep it in your cellar with the rest of your enormous wine collection."

"It'd be like finding a specific strand of hay in a haystack." Jack finished his glass of champagne. "Besides, the good stuff doesn't stay long enough to become evidence."

"Liar. With twins like yours, I'd wager it takes all day to finish a glass of wine. You need a wife."

Jack crossed his arms. "I do not."

"You are the very definition of a man in want of a wife. Wealthy, unmarried, in possession of two incorrigible brats—"

"*Adorable* brats."

"—a large home in need of a mistress—"

"I have a housekeeper."

"—and perhaps a few more maids capable of plaiting hair—"

"My entire staff can plait hair, from the cook to the butler," Jack informed him imperiously. "I taught them myself."

"*Wife*," Redmire repeated. "Get one."

"I had one." Jack's throat was suddenly too tight. "That's how I ended up with twins. She's gone. We're not going through that again."

He hadn't married her so she could manage his household. He'd married her for love. The only reason he'd marry anyone. Their union had been perfect. First the two of them, then the four of them, living in bliss.

And then came typhus.

The same year that Napoleon lost more soldiers to typhus than were killed by the Russians, much smaller epidemics had blossomed closer to home. Jack's children had been spared. His wife Sally had not. No matter how much blood the doctor had let or how much antimony he'd administered, Sally only grew weaker and weaker and eventually never opened her eyes again.

"Many people go their whole lives without love," he said quietly. "I was lucky enough to find mine and unlucky enough to lose her. There's nothing to search for. I had my time, and it's over."

"I didn't say 'love,'" Redmire said gruffly. "I said 'wife.' But any woman would do. You could do with one in your life, and I'd wager your children could, too."

"My children," Jack replied, "refuse to consider the idea. On the occasions in which they have witnessed attempted flirtations by young ladies in town, they informed me quite emphatically that they shall not countenance a substitute. Besides, I've no wish to remarry."

No wish to tear open the raw wounds of his heart to allow someone new inside. Someone who might grow to fill the empty spaces, to bring light where there was darkness, only to be ripped away anew, leaving his and his children's tattered hearts more decimated than before.

If he'd learned anything about love, it was that it didn't last. Once was enough.

"Forget marriage," Redmire said. "But you need *someone*. Do the twins at least have a governess?"

"They do not."

Before the typhus came, Sally had been teaching the children herself. After she died, the children had cleaved to Jack, begging him never to seek a "replacement mother" out of fear they wouldn't have as much time with their father anymore.

When Jack was young, he had no governess. He wanted his children to eventually have a better education than he'd had, but he also didn't wish to rob them of their childhoods. Sally and he had decided that once the twins turned ten, it would be time for formal education. Until then, the children could be children and she'd teach them herself.

Except it hadn't happened like that. Sally was gone. The twins were ten. There was no plan for formal education in place.

Jack spent every moment he could either playing with them or teaching them, but as Redmire had pointed out, Jack was just one person. Balancing his time between providing for his twins and being there for them was hard enough without—

"Blast your hide," he said with a sigh. "I need a governess."

"Next question." Redmire refilled their glasses. "Who?"

"I have no idea."

But an idea was beginning to form.

He could attack this problem the same way he solved shipping logistics. Whenever there were holes in one's knowledge, the most expedient way to fill them was to pose a question to someone who knew the answer.

Jack didn't know any governesses. He no longer even knew any single young ladies.

Except for one.

Mademoiselle Désirée le Duc was the younger sister of messieurs Sébastien and Lucien le Duc—Cressmouth's only blacksmiths, and Jack's favorite billiards opponents. Everyone with a carriage, sleigh, or child wishing to trundle an iron hoop passed through their smithy.

Désirée would be friends with other young ladies. If there was an out-of-work governess in the village, she might know about it. Although she herself was not in the market for genteel employment—frequently labeled "the most beautiful woman in Cressmouth," Jack was rather surprised she hadn't been swept to the altar by now—Désirée would at least have an idea of where to start.

Some friend of a friend was bound to be a governess, or have employed a governess, or be related to a governess... This could be a lot easier than Jack had feared.

"You're making the face," Redmire said. "You have a plan."

Jack abandoned his champagne and pushed to his feet. "I have a plan."

CHAPTER 2

*M*ademoiselle Désirée le Duc shoved a flyaway tendril of golden-brown hair back up under her drooping bonnet and returned to harvesting the last fruits of her garden. Soon the weather would be too cold, and the land would lie dormant until the spring. But today, the soil yielded two plump aubergines, a handful of courgettes, and half a basket of onions.

Lucien had forbidden her from working in the garden. It was gauche. A task for servants, not ladies. *He* was the one who should be making sacrifices. But like her brothers, Désirée also tended to ignore any proscription that stood in the way of providing for her family. What harm could there be in a vegetable garden? It gave her something to tend, to be responsible for, to be proud of. It fed her family. It was also her way to both help and rebel against brothers adamant their beloved sister never resort to manual labor.

Hiring a maid for this task made little sense. Not when the goal was to pay off this plot of land in order to return to France as soon as possible. Lucien and Bastien might not allow her to contribute in the smithy, but absolutely no harm would befall her out here in the—

"*Aie!*" A stray thorn had managed to scrape her forearm, raking the skin and leaving a thin line of blood in its wake.

Not the end of the world, except she was late for Lucien's English lessons, and he was bound to notice and cause a row. She wiped the blood against a clean spot on her apron and pushed to her feet. If she made haste, she could change from her gown into something with longer sleeves, and still get to the drawing room in time for lessons.

She hooked the basket over her other arm and hurried toward the house.

"Ho, there, Désirée," Uncle Jasper shouted as she rounded the corner. "What's for supper tonight?"

"You will find out when I make it," she called back with a smile.

The le Duc household was perennially short on servants. There was a footman who doubled as butler, and a pair of hardworking maids, but the only "chef" was the family pig Uncle Jasper was currently feeding.

Technically, the pig was not meant to be a pet named Chef, but rather a meal to eat. They were fattening him from a tiny piglet to meat that would last several weeks. But Désirée had developed a soft spot for poor Chef, and refused to entertain thoughts of slaughter.

Possibly because, most days, Chef was the only company she had.

Désirée ducked into the house via the rear entrance, dropped her basket of vegetables in the kitchen, then dashed to her bedchamber. After removing her apron and bonnet and changing gowns, she raced to the front parlor, feet sliding on the carpet-less floor, until she all but tumbled into the parlor out of breath and only… *mon Dieu*. Thirty minutes late?

Lucien glanced up from the worn sofa where he sat, his hazel eyes piercing.

"Tu es en retard."

"I know I am late," she answered in slow, crisp English. "But I am here now."

"C'est trop tard."

"No, it is never too late to learn something new," she replied, misunderstanding him on purpose.

At two-and-thirty—and the patriarch of

their family—Lucien did not think himself too old to learn English. He didn't see the point. Soon, they would be returning to France, and would never need to know a word of English again.

Soon. Soon, soon, soon. Perhaps Lucien required French lessons as well. He had been promising a *"rapide"* return for eighteen years. If she had not taught herself English, she would be even more isolated than she was now.

As isolated as Lucien no doubt felt.

She opened his exercise book and flipped to the last page. "Did you finish the preparation?"

"C'est stupide," he grumbled. But, yes, he had done it. And very well, by the look of it.

"Well done."

Although her brother tended to respond in French, regardless of the language in which he had been addressed, the accuracy and relevancy of his replies indicated he comprehended most of what was said. Rarely was he forced to ask a sibling to translate for him.

Coaxing him to *answer* in English was another *paire de manches*. He hated being seen as less-than-competent at any task. Having the thickest accent of the trio did not help.

What might help was actually practicing the language. Out loud. In a benign environment. One hour every afternoon, right here, with his *petite sœur.* Her brothers worked so hard, and never let her contribute. At least she could do this. She *liked* tutoring. Her brother, on the other hand…

"You should not be teaching me English," he said. "You should be improving your French."

Désirée had been nine years old when they'd been forced to flee their home. Old enough that she would probably never completely lose her native accent, but young enough that her French fluency was… well, only somewhat better than that of a nine-year-old. There were no French tutors in Cressmouth.

Except for these one-hour English lessons, she and her brothers exclusively spoke French around the house, which only expanded her vocabulary to the sorts of topics one might discuss with one's blacksmith elder brothers over the dinner table. Horses, carriages, food, fashion. How much better life would be when they were back in France where they belonged.

Désirée wasn't certain she belonged anywhere.

Well, other than "with her brothers," no matter what. Family came first. They had been through so much together. Every single one of them would do whatever it took to keep what was left of their family together.

So *of course* she was borrowing every possible French book from the castle lending library, in order to improve her French. Not because she feared embarrassing her brothers, but because from the bottom of her heart, she wanted more than anything to fit in. Not just to return to her ancestral home, but to *belong* there.

"You missed one." She underlined a badly conjugated verb and passed the exercise book back to Lucien. "What do you think belongs there?"

He pushed the exercise book away. "*C'est inutile.*"

"It is not pointless. Details like conjugation and word order can cause us to misunderstand others, or to be misunderstood. Did you see the new books I brought you?"

Lucien glared at her. "*Ils sont pour des enfants.*"

"They're for children, yes, or for adults who are learning a new language. I must have read these volumes a hundred times when I was studying English."

"You were a child," he grumbled in French. "You are still a child."

"I am seven-and-twenty. If you had attempted to learn back when I had started—"

"I wanted to leave." He shoved his dark hair

out of his eyes. "We wouldn't still be here if it weren't for Uncle Jasper."

"You are right," she said softly. "We would be dead."

That was the crux of the problem. Uncle Jasper was not a blood relative, but a family friend. At the height of the revolution, when being French aristocracy meant one's only trip was to the guillotine, Jasper had claimed three terrified orphans as his family and smuggled them into England.

The bargain he had made with Mr. Marlowe, owner of the castle on the hill and the village's founder, had seemed a godsend at the time. Rather than becoming tenants, subject to eviction at the whim of the landowner, Uncle Jasper owned this plot of land free and clear—provided he finished repaying its loan within twenty years.

Two years remained. Uncle Jasper, who had fed them and sheltered them and taught them everything there was to know about racing horses and running a smithy, could no longer work. He suffered gout so severe that most days, he could not even walk out back to toss Chef a few scraps from the kitchen.

More to the point, Uncle Jasper was English. He would not return to France even if his swollen limbs allowed it. And if Désirée and her brothers left now, before the lease was paid in full, the property would revert to the castle, leaving Uncle Jasper homeless and penniless.

He had saved them. They would not go home until they had saved him, too.

Lucien sighed. "It's just…"

"I know." She lay her head on his shoulder. "Fontainebleau."

He nodded, his big hands curling into fists.

For years, returning home had been couched in *one day* and *when the war ends*. But ever since the Treaty of Fontainebleau in April, *one day* had suddenly become *today*. Napoleon Bonaparte had been captured. The war was over. The day they'd been dreaming of was finally here.

France was where they had lost everything, and where Lucien believed they would find it again. They could return home whenever they liked.

Or at least, as soon as they repaid an exorbitant loan and saved up enough extra coin for both the journey, and a new life. You know. Just that, nothing more.

A shadow appeared in the doorway. It was their footman, Pinfield.

"*Excusez-moi, monsieur, madame.*" He cleared his throat. Although he tried, Pinfield was not French. They did not hold it against him. "Mr. Skeffington has arrived."

"He's early!" Lucien leapt up from the sofa with comical alacrity, leaving his English books where they lay. "Has the baize been ironed?"

Pinfield paled and sent a beseeching look toward Désirée.

"The billiard table," she said in English. "Has the baize been ironed?"

The footman's shoulders sagged in relief. "Yes, mademoiselle. Everything is in order."

"Thank you, Pinfield." She turned to scowl at her brother. "Don't tease him so. Your billiards vocabulary in English is as good as mine."

His hazel eyes widened innocently. *"Moi? Mais, je suis français."*

Yes, Lucien was a Frenchman, and the le Ducs possessed the only pocketless French-style billiards table in Cressmouth. *Carambole* had been the last treat Uncle Jasper bought them before his health kept him out of the smithy.

"Ladies take the first shot." Désirée raced her brother out of the parlor, knocking against him when they both tried to cram through the doorway at the same time.

When they reached the billiards room, the others were there waiting. Uncle Jasper was seated in the far corner, his heavy feet propped up high atop a stool. Her middle brother was handing him a glass of brandy, no doubt courtesy of their guest.

Rakish Sébastien was the fashionable le Duc sibling. Men called him Bastien, but the ladies called him Beau because they considered him the equal to Beau Brummell. Without the profligacy, of course.

Désirée tweaked Bastien's cravat—not because it was imperfect, but because touching its immaculate folds would vex her brother—and retrieved a cue from the closet. She busied herself with chalking the tip before turning to face Jack. She needed *something* in her shaking hands to belie how much he affected her.

Not because she cared what Jack Skeffington thought. Lucien would *throttle* her if he believed she fancied an Englishman.

Jack was, naturally, just as dashing tonight as he was on every other occasion in which she'd glimpsed him. Soulful dark eyes the color of fine chocolate. Too-long black-brown hair, a carelessly shaven jaw, a scar that drew her attention right back to those gorgeous, thick-lashed eyes...

"Good afternoon," he said in English.

Jack was Lucien's antithesis. Regardless of the language spoken to him, Lucien replied in French. And regardless of the language spoken to *him*, Jack replied in English. Somehow they managed to become the best of friends; thick as thieves.

Perhaps because they *didn't* speak the same language.

Or perhaps because they were, in fact, thieves.

In town, Jack was renowned for his impressive wine cellar. What the villagers did not know was that *les messieurs le Duc* aided Jack in his dealings with their countrymen in exchange for a percentage of the profits. In fact, if it weren't for Jack Skeffington, Désirée's family would not have held a prayer of paying off the loan in time to keep their property. He kept them informed during their monthly billiard matches, and each time their portion was even greater than the month before.

"There's brandy," he said.

"There's always brandy," she replied in French.

She suspected Jack understood French every bit as well as Lucien understood English, but refused to speak a word of it just to annoy her brothers. Désirée approved.

"There's also champagne, if you prefer." He gestured to a side table. "1811 Veuve Clicquot, if you're choosy about your vintage."

Désirée was not choosy. She also could not

have asked for better champagne, as he well knew.

"You are hoping that if I drink enough of this, you will finally win a game." But she poured herself a glass anyway. She loved champagne. This was what France would taste like when she returned home. Crisp and dry and bubbly.

"Teams," Bastien commanded in French.

Carom billiards was not properly played in teams, but because all four of them were formidable players, they had developed a way to stretch out the fun and make the scoring fairer. Four games, each played with two players, until each player from the first team had played both players from the second team.

Since all four of them were occasionally known to accumulate the required ten points to win the game on their first turn at the table, even this method did not last as long as some of the English games with pocket tables Désirée had witnessed at the castle.

But their way was more fun.

She bit her lip. It was time to choose a partner. "I choose…"

"Me," Lucien said. "Bastien, you're with Jack. Désirée, you take the first shot."

She downed her champagne before setting

the empty glass aside and settling into position. Going first was her favorite. If she was playing her brother, she would have finished in one turn. If she was playing Jack, she would take her time.

"*Qui m'oppose?* Jack? Bastien?"

"Me." Jack's dark eyes grinned at her above his glass of brandy. "Should I bother selecting a cue, or are you going to finish the game before I take a single shot?"

"Have a seat." She lined up her cue, then narrowed her eyes. "Where are your children?"

"Out in the garden with Chef."

"Poor Chef," Lucien murmured. "He wishes we'd cut him into *côtes de porc* after all."

"Don't worry," Jack assured him. "That's probably what the twins are doing."

See? Both obstinate *têtus* understood each other far better than they liked to let on.

Désirée rolled her eyes. "Pay attention to the table, please. Prepare to be amazed and astounded."

Jack leaned closer and lowered his voice. "What do you think about children?"

She missed her shot.

"I am amazed," said Lucien, deadpan.

Bastien nodded. "I am astounded."

Uncle Jasper, however, was fast asleep.

Désirée ignored all three and turned to face

Jack. "What do you mean, what do I think about children?"

"Mine," he clarified quickly. "Their education."

She frowned. "What's wrong with their education?"

"They haven't got one."

"Take your shot," Bastien called out.

Jack brandished his cue. And missed. Possibly because his eyes were on Désirée, rather than the table.

"You are seeking advice?" she asked. "From someone who has never birthed nor raised a child?"

"*Take your shot,*" Bastien groaned.

She did. Perfect point.

Jack's gaze was still on her. "I'm seeking advice from a young lady who I assume knows other young ladies. Do you know anyone with experience teaching children?"

Tutoring. She imagined any number of young women would leap at the chance to tutor Jack's children—if only because it brought them closer to Cressmouth's most eligible resident bachelor. But did she know anyone with actual experience teaching children?

"Désirée…" Lucien warned.

She took another shot. Another point.

Désirée had the same amount of child tutoring experience her friends did—which was to say, none at all. What she *did* have was a family in desperate need of money, and years of practice wrangling the three biggest *enfants* of all—Lucien, Bastien, and Uncle Jasper.

An idea tickled her skin. If she could cram English conjugation down Lucien's stubborn throat, certainly she could tutor Annie and Frederick in… whatever ten-year-olds needed tutoring in.

"You don't know *anyone* capable of teaching children?" she asked carefully.

Bastien leaned a hip against the table. "Désirée has plenty of experience with children. She tutors Lucien all the time. Weren't you saying you wished those lessons would stop? Here's your chance."

"The only thing I recall wishing to say," Lucien gritted out, "is that you can take this bright red ball and shove—"

"I'll do it," Désirée said decisively.

Jack startled backward. "You'll be their governess?"

"Their… what?" she stammered. *Governess* sounded significantly more involved than *tutor*. Then again, money was money. The faster they earned it, the sooner they could leave. "What kind of governess?"

Bastien poured himself a fresh glass of

brandy. "The 'teaches children' sort of governess, genius."

"No," said Lucien. "Absolutely not."

"It isn't manual labor," she pointed out. "Governesses are genteel."

"Not that it matters," Jack said with obvious confusion. "There aren't too many blacksmiths in High Society, either."

"Not helping," Désirée hissed.

"Whose shot is it?" Bastien asked.

Lucien glared at him. "Désirée's."

She pointed her cue. Another point. "Lucien, calm down and think rationally. It would not be 'real' work."

"Er…" Jack cleared his throat. "I feel I should disclose that my children are absolutely an enormous amount of work."

"No," Lucien said again.

"Ladies can do favors, can they not?" Désirée coaxed. "Perhaps volunteer, in exchange for pay?"

Bastien snorted. "That's not what 'volunteer' means."

"See?" Lucien pointed at Désirée. "Terrible governess. The answer is no."

Jack stepped so close she could smell the sandalwood at his throat. "So you're saying, in theory, that you might voluntarily donate some of your time, in exchange for me voluntarily donating some of my money?"

Lucien leapt to his feet. "You are *not* paying my sister for any favors!"

The insinuation should make her blush. Instead, she eyed Jack with interest. He might not think of *her* in that way, but she had on several occasions wondered what it would be like to—

"Désirée," Bastien barked. "Your turn."

This time, she blushed. And won another point. "Yes, to being a governess. I suggest a temporary arrangement in which—"

"Désirée will not accept work of any kind from any man." Lucien's eyes were thunderous. "She is a lady."

Bastien tilted his hand back and forth. "Or *would* be. Except she's not."

"*Will* be," Lucien enunciated. "After we return to France."

"Where they will have no idea whether I did or didn't tutor anyone's children whilst in England," Désirée pointed out. She made a pointed face that she hoped said, *Stop being arrogant. We need this money.*

Lucien's intractable expression said, *Over my dead body.* "This isn't one of your *remèdes* Désirée."

Jack blinked. " *Remèdes?*"

Bastien puffed up his chest with pride. "Her

31

remèdes are second to none. Our sister could find a way to make a bomb out of a fur muff and a hat pin."

Jack blinked a few more times. "Why would she need a grenade?"

"The grenade isn't the point," Désirée said quickly. "Resourcefulness is the point."

Because her English was better than Lucien's, she was the one who could take advantage of all the information stored in the castle library. Rather than read biographies and romances, she'd sought out practical volumes on simple mechanics. She'd never be mistaken for an engineer, but her *"remèdes"* had saved the family from countless situations.

"No," Lucien said. "The point is that I do not trust anyone alone with my sister. If you so much as look at her for too long, I will thrash you within an inch of your life."

Typical Lucien overreaction. Jack wasn't the one whose passions needed to be restrained. Désirée rolled her eyes toward Bastien, the brother of reason.

He nodded in understanding. "When Lucien's done thrashing you, I'll feed you to Chef. Pigs eat anything. Even Englishmen."

Uncle Jasper bolted upright with a broken snore. "Whose turn is it?"

"Mine." Désirée shot. Another point.

"Actually, I think you won three counts ago." Jack tilted his head, his dark eyes piercing hers. "Are you truly interested in helping my children?"

"Not forever," she admitted. "I could only be an interim governess. I shall return to France before your children are out of the schoolroom."

"That's right," Lucien said. "You cannot keep her."

"And," Désirée added, "if we are being completely honest... you may not even want me for the short term. I never had much formal education myself. Everything I learned after leaving France came from the castle library."

"Fair enough." Jack tapped the side of his chin, just beneath his scar. "You wouldn't be a *forever* governess. But right now, I'm not looking for an Oxford professor. I just need someone who knows more than my twins do, to get them started, while I look for a 'real' governess."

"Started?" Bastien repeated. "Do they not know their numbers and letters?"

"They're clever little slugs," Jack replied. "They can read, but choose not to."

"Spoiled," Lucien guessed.

"Dreadfully," Jack agreed. His face fell in obvious disappointment. "To be honest, the twins might be too much to handle."

"Désirée can handle a hog ten times her weight," Uncle Jasper said staunchly. "I've seen her."

"Désirée can race a high-flying phaeton better than any Englishman," Sébastien put in.

"Désirée can smelt iron, cook *galettes*, and break in wild horses," Lucien added hotly. "She can break your children, too."

All eyes swung to him.

"Wait," Désirée whispered. "Whose side are you on?"

"Yours," he muttered. "I won't allow anyone to doubt my sister." He winced. "I might have got carried away."

Jack clasped his hands together. "Splendid. My children love horses. We can all risk our lives together. Start the day after tomorrow, shall we?"

Swallowing hard, Désirée turned and held out her billiards cue toward Lucien. "*Mon grand frère*, it is your turn."

He stared at her for a long moment, then accepted the cue with a sigh. "Prepare to die, Bastien. I blame you for this."

"You blame me for everything," Bastien answered cheerfully. "Champagne?"

"That means I'll see you in two days,"

Désirée said to Jack, voice wobbling. Her stomach felt like wild horses had taken up residence and intended to kick their way out.

His slow answering smile only made her heart gallop faster.

There was no reason to be nervous, she assured herself. She'd head over every morning, force the twins to learn something, and be home by supper. Just until he found a true governess to replace her. If she could wrestle hogs and smelt iron, she could do this.

C'est de la tarte. Easy.

CHAPTER 3

"*A*nnie! Frederick!"

Jack's twins bounded out from the le Duc's rear garden with wind-flushed cheeks and matching grins.

"Frederick's afraid of pigs," Annie said as she fell into step beside her father.

"Am not," Frederick said hotly as he raced to Jack's other side. "You patted him like he was a dog!"

"Chef likes me." Annie sent him a smug smile. "We're friends."

Frederick lifted his chin. "I'll invite him over to eat your geese."

"You won't," Annie teased. "You didn't even go near him."

"He's filthy," Frederick protested. "Sébastien le Duc would never touch a pig. He's a fashionable gentleman."

"I'm glad I'm not a gentleman," Annie said with feeling. "They miss out on all the fun."

Jack declined to comment, instead choosing to enjoy the half-mile stroll home sandwiched between a ten-year-old would-be dandy and his joyfully unladylike sister.

As they tramped up the hill over a dusting of autumn leaves, the twins kept up a constant chatter, intermingled with shouts of good tidings and energetically waved hands whenever they passed a familiar face.

Which, in Cressmouth, was everyone. The twins knew every child old enough to toddle, and could greet every neighbor and shopkeeper by name. The Harpers, from whom they rented horses. Miss Church, whose family owned a dairy. Mrs. Pringle, who prepared the biscuit menu for the castle's welcome buffet. Miss Shelling, who wrote for the Cressmouth Gazette.

Was it any wonder neither Jack nor his offspring were inclined to ever leave this village? It was clean and safe, familiar and picturesque, with a soaring castle atop a frequently snow-topped mountain, surrounded by sloping hills of gorgeous evergreens. His children's home wasn't their cozy cottage in its acre of land abutting the central park, but the entire village.

Of course, playtime was about to become

significantly curtailed two days hence, when Désirée started coming over to instruct the twins in daily lessons. Er, that was to say, Mademoiselle le Duc. Jack would have to take care to speak in formal terms in front of the children, to underscore Désirée's position of respect.

Actually, he would have to take care, full stop. The last thing Jack wanted was a complicated liaison with a temporary governess. He didn't *think* her brothers would truly feed him to their pig over the slightest hint of untoward behavior, but all the same, the new arrangement would work best if all parties involved maintained impeccable comportment and respectability.

Annie stumbled against Jack's side with tears of laughter in her eyes. "Did you hear that, papa? Frederick can belch my name."

Very well, the *adults* would maintain proper decorum and the children would do... whatever the children would do. Oh, God, what were his children going to do?

Should he tell them now? No, not yet. They were having too much fun kicking clouds of yellow-orange leaves and chasing each other in circles around him, fingers outstretched in tickle position.

He would tell them after they arrived home,

once they were settled in for the nightly bed-time story. As they were too old for fairy tales— or so they'd informed him on their eighth birthday—he and the twins had just finished Robinson Crusoe and were now making their way through Gulliver's Travels.

Part of him couldn't help but feel like the family was about to embark on an adventure of their own.

"Can we cross through the park?" Frederick asked.

"We *have* to cross through the park." Annie stared at her brother as if he'd gone mad. "It's the only way to see my geese."

"Hurry *up*, papa." Frederick tugged Jack's elbow. "Sunset is the best time to see them. We're going to miss them."

Frederick was right. The horizon now matched the red-orange-yellow of the trees at the edge of the park.

Jack hurried up.

Once the geese were accounted for, and the children fed and readied for bed, he crawled in beside them, but did not immediately open the novel in his lap to tonight's chapter.

"What's wrong?" Annie asked.

"He's making the face," Frederick whispered. "The 'I have something to say and you're not going to like it' face."

Jack inclined his head in assent. "I need to have a discussion with you two."

"I'm sorry I teased Fred at hoops," Annie blurted out, at the same moment Frederick stammered, "I shouldn't have belched her name!"

"You're not in trouble," Jack assured them, although his smile felt hollow. If anyone was about to deliver a disappointment, it was him. He was both looking forward to and terrified by the idea of a woman under his roof, however platonically.

Earlier that year, when his children had been furious after witnessing a young lady make a flirtatious comment to their father during one of the castle assemblies, Jack had asked the twins if the idea of having someone new in their lives was truly so abhorrent.

Their answer had been an emphatic yes.

Of course, all three of them had been thinking the woman in question would be for Jack. This would be different.

As eye-achingly beautiful as Désirée le Duc might be, her visits would not be to see Jack, but to tutor his children. In fact, this was a step he should have taken long ago. He, like his twins, had been resistant to the idea of change, but changes would occur whether their family was prepared for them or not. A father's job was to equip his children as best he could.

"I have a wonderful surprise." Jack infused his voice with as much gaiety as he could. "You're going to be lucky enough to have a governess!"

"No," Annie said flatly.

Frederick crossed his skinny arms. "Absolutely not."

It was as if his children had learned the art of refusal at the feet of the grand master Lucien le Duc.

"*Yes*," Jack said firmly. "It's settled."

"It's not settled." Annie wrinkled her nose. "Do you know what kind of governess we'd like?"

"No governess," Frederick finished without hesitation.

Annie lifted her chin. "Exactly."

While it was lovely to see his children in agreement for once, this was not a fight they were destined to win. They needed an education. Jack could not devote his time to the business affairs that provided for their security and simultaneously spend his days at a slate in the schoolroom. Hence: governess.

But he did not want his children to feel they had no input into their own lives. So much had happened to them or been stolen from them that was outside their control. He never wanted them to feel that helpless again.

"Mademoiselle le Duc has agreed to act as temporary instructress while we hunt for a permanent governess. I have certain qualities in mind that the ideal candidate must fulfill, and I am certain the two of you will, too. We will make our final selection as a family. How does that sound?"

"Unnecessary." Annie crossed her arms to mirror her brother. "I don't need instruction. My friend Nigel says ladies aren't expected to know things."

Jack cleared his throat. What was the proper response here? That Nigel was a henwit? Or that Nigel was, in fact, absolutely correct that ladies were indeed not expected to know things, but a smuggler's daughter was never going to be a lady, therefore aristocratic foibles did not signify? *This* smuggler had no intention of raising a willfully ignorant daughter.

"It doesn't matter," Frederick mumbled to his sister. "No matter who it is, she won't stay."

Ah. There it was. The true reason his children were anti-governess.

Not because they assumed they wouldn't like her. But because they feared they wouldn't get to keep her. Just like they hadn't been able to hold on to their mother.

Jack's chest tightened. He wished he could swear to them that everyone who entered their lives was there to stay. That never again would they fall in love with someone, only to have a fever or an accident or a change of heart rip them away.

All three of them knew better.

They were right not to get attached. Governesses came and went. Their post was, by definition, temporary. Once the children learned all that they could learn or reached a certain age —that was it. Goodbye. Never to see each other again.

Yet they couldn't cloister themselves in the house, never allowing anyone in. He could not replace the mother they had lost, nor would he wish to try, but it was time the children learned that not all change was bad. *Life* was change.

"Tomorrow, we have a full day to spend however we like," he informed them softly. "The following day, you'll have your first lessons with Mlle. le Duc. You like her."

"She's not a real governess though," Frederick muttered. "A temporary friend."

Annie lightly punched his arm. "Maybe she doesn't want to spend all day with you."

He punched her back harder. "Maybe you're the reason she can't wait to go home."

"She's a... mostly... real governess," Jack said, his voice as firm as possible, given he was inventing his argument from whole cloth. "She's not running away from either of you. She's staying here until... until we find our *real*, real governess and don't need her anymore."

He hoped. He'd no doubt have to triple her salary to make it worth her time.

"She's staying all day and all night?" Frederick's eyes were huge. "Like a real governess would?"

"Yes, absolutely." Jack nodded. He'd quadruple her salary. Sextuple her salary. Whatever it took. "Like a real governess. She can't wait."

Annie narrowed her eyes. "Is she bringing her pig?"

"She is not bringing her pig." He tweaked his daughter's nose. "No pigs."

"It would eat the geese anyway," Frederick whispered.

Annie crossed her arms. "Not if the pig stayed in the house."

"No pigs in the house." Jack opened the book. "Ready for Gulliver's Travels?"

They snuggled against him.

"I can't wait to find out how he escapes the giant wasps," Annie said with an extra wiggle.

"Has it occurred to you," Jack suggested slowly, "that you could *read* the book to find out?"

Frederick shook his head. "If we read it ourselves, then you wouldn't need to come and do bedtime stories anymore."

Jack's heart twisted at the catch in his son's voice. It wasn't that his stubborn children didn't want to read. They were afraid to lose more time with the one parent they had left.

"A governess is a good thing," he told them. "Having lessons with her all day, means I can spend all evening with you. Whether you cheat and read ahead or not."

His children gazed at him for a long moment in silence, then exchanged a telling glance.

"We might have cheated," Annie admitted.

Frederick had the grace to blush. "We might already be in Part III, where his boat gets attacked by pirates."

Annie flipped ahead. "Turn to page one hundred and eighty-three."

"What are you scamps doing?" Jack protested. "*I* didn't cheat. What boat? What pirates? What happened to the giant wasps?"

He hid his grin as his rambunctious twins

talked over each other to passionately explain Gulliver's adventures with a monkey and an eagle and an audience with King Brobdingnag.

He hoped Désirée was more than a match for his family's madness.

live-in governess? Of all the absurd... How long could it possibly take to find and employ a *real* governess? Even if the answer was "weeks," how could Désirée walking over from half a mile away truly make the difference between her success or failure?

The answers did not matter, she reminded herself. It didn't even matter if there *weren't* any answers. What mattered was the breathtaking daily salary Jack was willing to offer if she went along with the full-time-governess charade. Each day would earn her family the equivalent of a week's wages. It was worth it.

It also meant Désirée had spent the entirety of the previous day preparing the house for her absence. Harvesting the last vegetables from the garden. Baking pies for Uncle Jasper, fresh bread and pastries for her brothers, returning overdue books to the castle lending library and borrowing a heavy stack of new ones for Lucien to read in her absence from the hundreds of books the Duke of Azureford had just donated to the castle.

There was even a new 'remède' for Chef—a special series of tubes leading from the scullery to his pen, so that scraps could reach him even if Uncle Jasper's gout was too painful to permit afternoon visits with the pig.

That was yesterday. All the easy things.

Today was for goodbyes.

It seemed ridiculous to become emotional and mawkish at the idea of moving a fifteen-minute walk away from one's family. But the truth was, Désirée had never spent a single night away from her brothers. They had been all each other had for so long that she doubted she could sleep under a different roof.

Leaving home made a tiny part of her feel like she was a terrified little girl again, fleeing France and everything she'd known and loved for a future she could neither predict nor control. Back then, at least she'd had her brothers. Starting today, she would just have… herself.

Bastien and Lucien were waiting for her by the front door.

"*I'm* driving you to Skeffington's." Bastien's posture was belligerent and his tone self-satisfied, as though he and Lucien had used their fists to determine which brother would play coachman and have the final goodbye.

"Go and put her trunk in the carriage," Lucien commanded.

Bastien paused, as though he might argue, then just as quickly changed his mind, hastening the battered leather case out the door.

It wasn't so much *Désirée's* trunk as the only receptacle they'd had opportunity to grab before fleeing their home. For several long, uncertain weeks, its contents constituted every item the le Duc children owned. Once they'd been installed in Cressmouth with Uncle Jasper, the no-longer-necessary trunk had been relegated to a forgotten corner of the attic.

Until now.

"You don't have to do this," Lucien said quietly.

Of course she did. They needed the money, and Désirée would do anything to keep her family safe and together.

"It's fine," she assured him. "It will only be a handful of days at most. Besides, I thought you *liked* taking money from Englishmen."

"Very much. I just didn't want you to have to resort to…" He winced as if tortured. "You had a dowry."

"I don't need a dowry."

"You would be married by now."

"I reject any husband who wishes to marry me for my dowry."

"It should still be yours." His gaze was fierce. "I swear to you, once we regain our lands and our birthright, I will give you your portion outright, and you may determine the use of every *sou* as you please. Spend it all on Bordeaux and Camembert, if you don't want a dowry."

Désirée's stomach growled. "I just might."

It sounded as much an impossible dream as the rest of it. Returning to France. Returning *home*. Recovering lost birthrights. She had been due a dowry, but Bastien and Lucien had been in line for a title. At the time, *distantly* in line. But when the revolution had turned violent...

"It won't be much longer," Lucien promised. "We are at most a year away from repaying the lease and securing Uncle Jasper's future. Then we will sail across the Channel and never look back."

A year, at most. Could it finally be true?

"That's no excuse to ignore the books I borrowed for you." She wagged a finger at him. "Read and study every day. They are not due to be returned for a fortnight."

"Be home by then," he said gruffly.

"Be fluent by then," she teased back. "*Grand*

frère, I must go. I shall be just down the road. If you need me…"

"If you need *anything,*" he answered, "my arms and my fists are both at your service."

She kissed his cheek and slipped out the door.

Bastien helped her into the carriage. "Did Lucien perform the 'you need not do this' speech?"

She arched her brows. "You aren't going to say the same?"

"Would it matter?" He took the reins. "You can and should do as you please. I have never met anyone more capable than *ma petite sœur*. If anything, I am surprised you did not invent a *'remède'* that would project your body into both places at once so that you could do Skeffington this favor without actually leaving home."

"Believe me," she said with a grin. "I tried. The best I could do was install tubes to deliver food to Chef. Now Uncle Jasper can be in two places at once."

The brisk autumn air braced her cheeks as her brother expertly steered their carriage up the winding road toward the Skeffington residence on the other side of the castle.

Bastien's grip on the reins grew tighter. "If he touches you…"

"He won't touch me," Désirée assured him.

Jack wouldn't come near her even if she asked him to. Englishmen were too frightened of her brothers' protective wrath to engage in occasional flirtatious banter, much less dare to steal a kiss.

Although she would never admit it to her brothers, Désirée had no such compunction. She wasn't going to *marry* an Englishman, for the love of *madeleines*. But what harm could there be in kissing one or two or three before returning to France and respectability?

The bonnet of the carriage grazed a few low-hanging branches as they cut through the park, sending a smattering of red and yellow leaves dancing into the air.

Bastien guided the horses away from the narrow stream that flowed through the rear garden of the Skeffington property and circled round to the front instead, stopping the carriage as close to the door as possible.

"This is temporary." His eyes held hers. "You will be an excellent governess."

She nodded, swallowed. "I will be an excellent temporary governess."

But now that they were here, the scheme felt more, rather than less fantastical. With the exception of Marlowe Castle—and the Duke of Nottingvale's palatial winter home, the rest of Cressmouth's residents lived in cozy cottages with stone chimneys and cheery red roofs.

Jack Skeffington's cottage somehow seemed more imposing than all the others. Perhaps it was larger than most. Or perhaps the vast gardens surrounding it made it seem more isolated than the others.

Or perhaps Désirée was suffering a preemptive attack of homesickness at the prospect of being apart from her brothers.

Bastien sighed. "I'll get your trunk."

She nodded.

But before either of them could alight from the carriage, the front door flew open and a trio of footmen spilled out. One helped Désirée down whilst the other two ferried her scarred leather trunk into the house and out of sight.

"Of course," Bastien muttered. "When we regain our birthrights—"

"—we'll have footmen for our footmen," she murmured back.

But the truth was, she wasn't thinking about footmen. Or France. Or even her brothers.

Jack Skeffington had just appeared on his front step.

Dark brown hair tumbled carelessly over his forehead, in contrast to the perfect folds of the brilliant white cravat flowering out from a crisp black jacket and a waistcoat the green of ocean froth on a summer day. He had the muscled legs of a talented rider, and the expensive but un-shined boots of a man who could afford anything he wanted... but did not waste his time with anything that did not truly matter.

He smiled at Désirée. "We've been looking forward to your arrival."

Annie and Frederick's eager faces poked out from either side of him.

"No pig," Annie said with obvious disappointment.

"I told you," Frederick said smugly.

"I brought something better," Désirée replied, and reached into the carriage for the two treats she'd set aside the day before, while baking for her family. "A piece of *mille feuille* for each of you."

The twins hesitated.

Belatedly, Désirée realized the household undoubtedly had its own non-porcine chef, who was more than capable of baking the children sugared treats anytime they pleased.

"If you dislike delicious pastries," she said, "I'll send these home to the pig."

"Am I the pig?" Bastien stage-whispered in English. "Please say I'm the pig."

The twins ran forward and snatched the squares of *mille feuille* from Désirée's hands before the treats were gone forever.

Jack sent them a stern look.

"*À bientôt*, little sister," Bastien said to Désirée in French. "I love you. We're here if you need us. If the children misbehave, dunk them in the stream."

"I will," she promised.

"They'd like that," Jack said with a sigh. "That's where the geese are."

"I'll think of something better," she assured him as her brother climbed back into his carriage and drove away.

The le Ducs always thought of something. They'd once had everything, then nothing, and were clawing their way back toward the top. A temporary post as interim governess was the least of what she'd do to restore her family back in France.

"Now for the tour." Jack led her up a flight of stairs. "Bedchambers are this way. The guest chamber is here to the left; your trunk is already inside. The children have the chamber opposite. There is an interior door connecting to what was once a separate nursery and is now their schoolroom, and it can also be reached from the end of that hall. My bedchamber is just beyond, and the staff quarters directly underneath."

He led her back down to the ground floor via a different staircase, taking her past the kitchen and scullery and the exit to the rear garden, on past his private office, to the grand dining room and comfortable parlors in the front of the house.

In one, the children sat before a fire, making quick work of the *mille feuille* Désirée had brought. The other drawing room was vacant of children, but contained an elegant tea tray set for two.

Jack gestured for Désirée to select the seat of her choice next to the fire.

"I'm told nine in the morning is too early for a visit to the wine cellar, so we'll save that for another day." His shameless grin indicated he visited his wine cellar any time he pleased. "I thought we might start lessons tomorrow, and today let you become familiar with your new accommodations and more comfortable around the children."

"Very thoughtful," Désirée murmured as she poured herself a cup of tea.

In fact, everything Jack had done so far had been extremely thoughtful. She shouldn't be surprised. The prescient attention to detail that made him one of the country's most successful smugglers of French brandy was likely the same characteristic that made him a competent manager of his household and an excellent father.

"Your children don't seem upset to have a usurper in their midst," she commented.

"They're not upset *anymore*," he admitted wryly. "As unimpressed as they originally were, they took the news much better than I had feared, given how violently they oppose the idea of a stepmother." He widened his eyes. "Perhaps recounting *Children's Tales* from the Brothers Grimm was a bad idea."

She dropped a lump of sugar into her tea. "You speak German?"

"You know the book?" he asked in surprise.

"The castle lending library just received a copy. Virginia translated the title for me, and I returned it to the shelf."

"Excellent choice." He nodded approvingly. "Exactly what I should have done. Or at least refrained from calling the twins *Hänsel* and *Grethel* when they misbehave. If ever you come across a lovely cottage made of gingerbread and spun sugar... *Run*."

"Sage advice." She pantomimed taking notes in a journal. "I shall add that to the list, right after 'spiders' and 'warm ratafia.'"

He gasped in horror. "Who doesn't like spiders?"

"Everyone." She shivered daintily. "If your children do not already possess a solid phobia, that will become our first lesson."

"Then it sounds like you have the curriculum well in hand. Let's discuss the timetable. How about lessons from nine to noon, then again from two to six, breaking once for tea? You would be encouraged, but not required, to join us in the dining room for meals. Sundays would be yours to do as you please."

"That is more than fair." Désirée wasn't certain whether to be thrilled at the unexpected day off every week, or disappointed at the commensurate loss in income. Then again, she had been thinking of her stay in terms of days rather than weeks. "How long do you suppose it will take to find a proper governess?"

"I don't know," he replied, his expression honest. "I've never tried before. Finding you was significantly easier than expected. If I keep up this pace, you might be back home before teatime."

She lifted her cup. "We are having tea right now."

"Good God." He affected great consternation. "What are you still doing here?"

"Wasting as much time as possible," she replied without hesitation. "I'm milking you for money in order to finance my family's return home to France."

"Are you returning?" he asked with interest.

"As soon as we can." She rubbed her arms.

"We've been here for eighteen years, so it's not going quite as swimmingly as your governess hunt."

He inclined his head. "I've heard revolutions and war have a way of changing one's plans."

"Indeed." She lifted a Shrewsbury Cake from the tea tray. "What is it I am to do when I am not imparting invaluable lessons to your children?"

"Anything you like. There are floors to scrub, laundry to wash, vegetables to peel…" He frowned. "I am teasing, of course! The staff handles such things. I will not impose upon your free time. My plan is to work during the day whilst the children are at lessons, then spend my evenings spoiling them shamelessly."

With a man like this, Désirée had no doubt Jack meant to spoil his children not with money and presents, but with his time. All he wanted was whatever was best for his children. She could not help but admire a father like that.

Annie and Frederick appeared in the doorway.

"The pastries are gone," Frederick said in a devastated, end-of-the-world tone Désirée might have used to lament… well, the absence of available dessert, for one. She and the children clearly had much in common.

"Would you like to show me your school room?" she asked.

"No." Annie lowered her voice. "That's where the books are."

Frederick nodded. "Papa might notice we skipped ahead to the bit where Gulliver's crew commits mutiny."

Jack clasped his hands to his chest as though he'd been struck with an arrow. "You rascals peeked ahead? *Again?*"

Annie turned curious eyes to Désirée. "What do *you* like to read?"

Travel journals about France. Illustrated guides on the workings of clocks or ovens or how to remove stubborn stains from good fabric.

"No books containing delicious German sugar cottages," she assured them. "Unless you enjoy…"

"Being murdered and eaten?" Frederick suggested.

Désirée turned to Jack in horror. "*This* is your idea of a bedtime story?"

"The title was *Children's Tales*," he protested.

"Children who are tortured and killed in clever ways," Annie agreed. "Locked in a tower…"

"Eyes pecked out by crows…" Frederick added.

"Cutting off their own toes in order to fit their foot into a glass slipper…"

"Who wouldn't have sweet dreams after that?" Désirée asked faintly. "Enough literature. What do you like to do when you're not suffering horrible nightmares?"

"Horses," Annie answered at once. "Papa promised we could go riding today."

Frederick's eyes brightened. "Are you coming with us?"

"I would love to," Désirée said warmly. "I adore horses."

"We like to race them," he warned. "You must try hard to keep up."

"I shall do my very best," she promised.

"My grandfather used to raise horses," Jack explained. "Decades ago, he sold his best stud to the Harpers' stud farm. Once a week, that's where we go riding."

Désirée was familiar with the Harpers' farm. Like the le Duc smithy, it stood just on the outskirts of Cressmouth proper. She and her brothers had raced horses and carriages with the Harpers on many memorable occasions.

It was bizarre to visit not with her own family, but with someone else's.

In no time, she and the three Skeffingtons were settled on rented mounts at the mouth of one of many trails leading through the evergreens.

"Go!" Frederick shouted and flew off down the path.

"Beast." Annie disappeared right behind him in a cloud of dust and autumn leaves.

Jack did not go. He brushed off his hands and consulted his pocketwatch. "The twins won't be back until supper time. That gives us three childless hours. We can take this opportunity to eat ices in the castle common room without telling them, or I can nip over to the barber for a quick trim about the ears, or we could—"

Désirée interrupted him. "I'll race you to the curve leading to the main road."

"Go!" Jack bolted away in ungentlemanly fashion, just as his son had done, without waiting for her to prepare.

She did not need to prepare. Désirée and her brothers had spent most of their eighteen years in Cressmouth racing up and down these very woods. She could win this race with a wooden hobby-horse.

Grinning, she gave her horse his head and tore down the colorful path behind her employer.

To her surprise and delight, she did not catch up with Jack until the curve was in sight.

He made the mistake of glancing over his shoulder to gauge the distance between them, which gave her just enough time to spur her mount the last few yards.

Their horses reached the bend nose-to-nose.

Jack and Désirée stared at each other in disbelief, panting just as much as their horses and grinning at each other like simpletons.

"I was going to let you win," he managed. "Until I realized you were going to thrash me in the most humiliating way possible unless I tried my utmost."

"I was going to let *you* win," she admitted once she caught her breath. "Masculine pride being such a fragile little flower and all. But you were barely a second ahead and already I could not see where you'd gone and… here we are."

There they were. Neither had won.

She could not help but wonder if it was an omen.

CHAPTER 5

*D*ésirée hunched over an escritoire in the corner of her guest chamber, thumbing through the castle lending library's latest collection of French fashions. The mysteries contained within seemed more crucial to learn than any subject taught in a school room.

Now that she and her brothers were no longer in danger of losing their heads by returning home, the question had changed from *what if we never get there* to *what will I do when we do?*

What if they did succeed in reclaiming their land? What if Désirée did have her choice between a life of leisure or an eye-watering dowry? What if Lucien did inherit a title or what if she won the heart of some wealthy French aristocrat, and suddenly needed not just to *look* the part, but *be* the part?

She wanted to acquit herself as brilliantly as possible. To make her brothers and herself proud. Even if that meant spending the next year studying every bit of literature or news or fashion she could get her hands on.

A knock sounded on her bedchamber door. "Mademoiselle?"

Désirée turned to face young Hester, who had been acting as lady's maid rather than chambermaid. Yet another temporary thing in a house full of temporary things.

"Yes, Hester?" Why was she here? It was too early to dress for bed.

"Mr. Skeffington would like to invite you to join him for a glass of wine."

Désirée blinked. "He would?"

Hester nodded.

"Now?"

Hester nodded.

"In the dining room?"

Hester shook her head. "In the wine cellar."

His *private* wine cellar. His renowned, exaggerated, much-whispered-about utopia of bottled ambrosia, which few had ever seen. The Skeffington wine cellar was rumored to have more French wine than France itself.

"Of course I want a glass of wine," she managed, despite her scratchy throat.

Hester twisted her hands. "Do you want me to dress your hair?"

Désirée hesitated. *Was* she being invited to a glass of wine? Or was she being invited to share something else entirely? Did he see her as something more than Bastien and Lucien's little sister?

"Yes," she said emphatically. "Please dress my hair."

She wished she had a fashionable gown. Or that they hadn't had to sell their mother's jewels in order to avoid living on the streets.

But a serviceable gown with unadorned hair and nothing decorating her earlobes or wrists or neck would simply have to do. It was all she had.

She closed the book of fashion plates upon her escritoire and crossed to the dressing table, where Hester was selecting curling tongs to heat in the fire. How much easier this was when one did not have to curl the back of one's hair by oneself! Désirée settled into the indicated velvet stool before the looking glass.

"Are you comfortable here?" Hester asked.

It took a moment for Désirée to realize Hester referred not to the plush dressing stool, but here in her new position; here in this house.

"Yes," she was forced to admit. "Very much."

After three full days as temporary governess,

the strangest aspect of her new circumstances was not one she would have predicted.

The twins were full of energy and curiosity, making lesson times a delight. She took meals with Jack four times a day—breakfast, luncheon, teatime, supper—but never unchaperoned. The children always flanked them. Even having servants at every possible post had taken an embarrassingly short period of time to get used to. Not having to grow her own vegetables or iron her own gowns was a hedonistic pleasure.

No, the strangest part of living in a different home with different rules and different food and different people was having to do so in *English*.

Before becoming the Skeffingtons' temporary governess, Désirée had, on some level, believed herself not to be fully French. Having every single thing that happened to her occur exclusively in English made it all the stranger and more dreamlike.

That she was *not* English was confirmed on the very first day, when ten straight hours of the language had given her a thunderous megrim. The second day, with *twelve* straight hours of English, had not fared much better. On the third day, however, she had caught herself thinking in English several times, even when no one was speaking it to her.

And now, day four—*le quatrième jour, s'il te plait*—her head no longer ached, and entire hours passed without her consciously noticing that they had done so in another language.

The feat was both thrilling and terrifying.

Do not get used to this, she reminded herself in French. *None of it.*

Not the language, not the home, not the servants, not the children.

She and the twins did everything together. They practiced penmanship, chased frogs, identified prime numbers, devised *"remèdes"*, made crowns of flowers, memorized countries and kings and capitals. They were as rapacious and rambunctious as her own siblings, and just as easy to love.

Désirée could not allow such a disaster to occur.

She was temporary. They were Skeffingtons and she was le Duc. She had to keep her emotional distance for their sake as much as hers. She was not their mother. She was not even their real governess.

All of them had already known far too much loss to wish for another painful farewell.

"There." Hester set down the curling tongs in satisfaction. "You are an angel."

Désirée was far from an angel. She was

looking forward far too much to finding out what surprises the rest of the evening might hold.

Softly flickering sconces lined the staircase leading down into the cellar. Despite the presence of a small fireplace, it was much cooler belowstairs, likely to mind the temperature of the wine.

Shelf after shelf of endless glass bottles seemed to stretch into infinity. It had been years since Désirée had last stood in a vineyard, but she'd wager the quantity seen here rivaled the quantity she'd seen there—and likely rivaled the quality, as well.

So taken was she with the astonishing array of wines, she did not at first notice the decorated table near the small fire... or the handsome man rising to greet her.

Even in the dim light, Jack's eyes sparkled. "What do you think?"

"I think you could drink a bottle with every meal and two before bed and still never finish them all," she replied in awe.

He grinned at her. "Let's try it. You pick first."

"I cannot." She turned in a slow circle. "I would not know where to start."

"Are you of a humor for Italian *chianti*, Spanish *rioja*, or—"

"French," she said decisively. "Something French."

He strode deeper into the cellar. "White? Red?"

"Perhaps a varietal from a young merlot berry with subtle oak undercurrent and a rich aroma reminiscent of plum and cherry."

Jack stopped and spun to look at her, nonplused. "You know wine?"

"I know Bordeaux," she said with a grin. "My family's land included vineyards along the Garonne."

"You grew up on a vineyard?"

"I spent every autumn in a *chateau* whose land included vineyards." She'd toured every day at her father's side, dreaming of the day she would have a vineyard of her own.

He practically licked his lips. "I could not be more envious. I *dream* of living on a vineyard."

"Unless you also dream of having it stripped from you the day your parents are hauled off and executed in front of the entire town, perhaps I am not the one to envy," she said. "I have not been on that vineyard in many, many years. But if you have something like that, it might taste like home."

Silence surrounded them for a tense moment, and then Jack pointed off toward the fire.

"Sit," he commanded. "Allow me to bring

you a glass of your childhood. The finest in my collection."

She sat. The chairs here in the cellar were even softer and more welcoming than the satin-finished *chaises longues* in his front parlor. Although the fire was small, its beauty and warmth combined with the chairs' elegance and comfort to beguile its visitor into sitting and relaxing, and likely having another glass, and another.

"Here." Jack handed her a crystal glass and poured an inch of thick red liquid. "If this is not the one, say the word, and I will open every bottle I have until we find it."

She swirled the wine in her glass, marveling at its gorgeous texture and the way it shimmered in the firelight. Then she lifted the rim of the glass to her nose and inhaled.

Cedar and wet clay, as smooth and balanced as she remembered. She brought the glass to her lips and took a sip. The flavor coated her tongue, her throat, her heart. She closed her eyes and let it flow through her. It was not exactly her parents' vineyard, but it was very, very close. It tasted like a favorite memory: a copy of the real thing, but the best she could have.

"Yes," she whispered. "Thank you."

He filled her glass, then set the bottle on her

side of the table before reaching for a different bottle of wine.

She jerked in surprise. "You do not wish to drink something so perfect?"

"It's yours." His eyes crinkled. "I won't rob you of a single moment's pleasure."

"You shan't be." She pushed the bottle toward him. "I cannot share my family's vineyard with you, but we can share this."

His eyes met hers. "All right. I would like that."

She watched him pour a glass. "I suppose there is a funny story about how this wine ended up in your collection."

"There is an exploit attached to each bottle in this cellar," he admitted. "Some anecdotes more humorous than others. I obtained this particular bottle during my last voyage at sea."

"When you gave up being a water smuggler for a land smuggler?"

"When I stopped being a privateer and became a papa," he corrected. "Well, that and a patron of ethically murky international trade. Which, if you're interested, pays better than the government pays its privateers."

"Unless you do both?"

"Exactly." His eyes closed as he took his first sip. "The war has not been easy on anyone. Many rural villages are shockingly poor. By paying them handsomely to help guide bottles like this one from the coast to whichever corner of England it's needed, they can subsidize their wages and revitalize their local economy."

"It is practically a public service," she murmured.

He nodded. "I should be knighted."

"You may not have heard this," she said, "but war also has a demoralizing effect on one's constitution. Wine, on the other hand—"

"And brandy!"

"—and champagne… *these* are the indispensable medicines that can sustain a functioning society in hard times."

He grinned at her. "After this governess bit, you might consider a career as a privateer. Or in politics."

"And you might consider purchasing a vineyard."

"I do consider," he said fervently. "Every hour of every day. I have an imaginary farm that lives only in my head. I'm forever planting and bottling and labeling and tasting. It's exhausting, and it's not even real."

"Why don't you start one, then?"

"Besides the exhaustion?"

She nodded. "Besides that."

"It's too cold here. Cressmouth is winter eight months of the year. It's beautiful and festive and Christmassy, but not conducive to planting grapes."

"You could move," she pointed out.

He shook his head. "Not until my children are grown and married. They love it here, and frankly it's a parent's delight. Scores of children to play with, without the dangers of crime and traffic. Everyone knows each other and helps each other. There are activities year-round; an entire castle at the village's disposal. Most importantly, Annie and Frederick have no desire ever to leave."

She set down her glass. "You asked?"

"I asked." He gave her a crooked smile. "They were singularly unimpressed with my 'what about grapes' argument."

She grinned back. "They do seem hard to impress."

"Not so." He leaned back. "They tell me you perform some sort of scientific magic tricks they've christened *le ducs*."

"Neither science nor magic, I'm afraid. Just tricks my brothers refer to as *'remèdes.'* I made my first when I was the twins' age. I wanted to be able to toast more bread without rising from the dining table, so I created a system of levers and pulleys… that very nearly burned down our dining room."

"Oh, good." He clapped his hands. "You're teaching them practical skills."

She laughed. "I got better. And wilier. Your children think we create our afternoon *'remèdes'* for fun, but secretly they are learning about physical properties and mechanics."

"Positively Machiavellian." He topped off their glasses. "I approve."

"At least someone appreciates my *remèdes*." She lifted a shoulder good-naturedly. "I am fairly certain Lucien and Bastien are simply resigned to them."

"Talk about hard to impress... People all over England flock here to Cressmouth and your family can't wait to leave."

"What we truly want," she corrected softly, "is to turn back the clock. It is too late, but we still must try to retrieve anything we can."

He met her gaze, his expression serious. "I cannot imagine how hard it must have been. How hard it still is."

"Many little things," she agreed. "I was born in the south of France and grown in the north of England. I feel replanted. Neither fully French, nor fully English. I am one of your grapes, frozen in the wrong region."

"It would be terrible not to be able to go home." He set his glass aside and leaned forward. "But is there nothing here you like?"

She bit her lip, then whispered, *"English pies.* Do not tell Lucien."

He chuckled, his laughing eyes less than a foot away from hers. "You'll set your dining room on fire, cross the English Channel, race neck-or-nothing through treacherous woods... but you won't tell your brother you like English pies?"

"That isn't all I like." She licked her lips.

He noticed.

She did it again.

His voice was scratchy. "Désirée..."

She set her wine aside. It tasted like home; but she did not long for home right now. She wanted something much, much closer.

"I..." He jerked away, flinging himself back into the recesses of his chair. "Should definitely not do what I've spent far too much time thinking about doing. Forgive me."

She would forgive him, but only because his words lit a forbidden flame.

He wanted her, too.

CHAPTER 6

*J*ack usually spent the quiet hours between dawn and the moment his children awakened outside either on his own acre of land or, like this morning, wandering the castle's sprawling public park. Nature was usually calming, relaxing, rejuvenating... Not today.

He'd almost kissed her.

God, how he'd wanted to. Sometime in the past two years, Désirée le Duc had gone from being the beautiful, untouchable, younger sister of Jack's business associates and billiards opponents, to *I-don't-care-seems-worth-it-come-here-and-kiss-me.*

The billiard games were no longer an excuse to drink good wine whilst discussing the finer points of his smuggling venture, but an excruciating exercise in pretending he had any interest

81

at all in winning the game when all his eyes wanted to take in was Désirée.

Not just his eyes. His mouth, his hands, his ears. She was clever and kindhearted, wild and funny. She raced phaetons, baked *mille-feuille*, solved problems with tubes and pulleys... How could anyone be indifferent to someone like that?

The only reason he'd managed to mask his interest for this long was because he'd believed his secret desires to be one-sided.

Apparently... they were not.

Jack tilted back his head and stared up at the endless sky. Désirée being one-hundred-percent amenable to a bit of no-questions-asked kissing was both the best thing and the worst thing that could have happened.

He would never remarry. He had no wish to complicate his life with an affair. And even if nothing more untoward occurred than a single stolen kiss...

Was anything ever "just a kiss?"

"Good morning, Mr. Skeffington!"

He spun to discover Miss Margaret Church and Miss Eve Shelling strolling up the opposite path. No doubt he'd painted quite a picture, head back, palms open, beseeching the heavens for any sign of what he should do.

"Good morning, ladies. How do you do?"

"My new boots pinch my toes," Miss Shelling confessed. "I think no more walking for the rest of the day."

"At seven o'clock? You'll need to find more comfortable shoes by Monday." Miss Church turned toward Jack with a smile. "Don't forget, you promised to come wassailing with us."

"*And* you promised to provide wassail," Miss Shelling added. "The only reason half our friends agreed to go caroling is because we'll be starting at the house with the best wassail."

"A gentleman keeps his promises," Jack said gravely. "And so do I."

They grinned at him. "See you Monday!"

Miss Shelling hobbled off, waving away Miss Church's attempts at support.

Perhaps ill-fitting shoes were good practice for Monday. After a cup or three of potent wassail, not all of the carolers would manage to walk in a straight line.

He turned back toward his property. Soon, his children would be rising. He and Désirée needed to have a serious conversation first. She was the teacher. He was the parent. She was the employee. He was the employer.

No kissing.

Jack strode back inside his home with a renewed sense of purpose... and absolutely no idea where to find his children's temporary governess.

She wasn't with the twins. Or in her chambers. Or the dining room.

It wasn't until he gave up the search and wandered into the kitchen to spoil his breakfast with one of Cook's lemon tartlets that he inadvertently stumbled across Cook and Désirée both, their heads stuck in the oven.

"What," he asked politely, "are you madwomen doing?"

Their heads popped out of the oven at once.

"Oh." Désirée's cheeks flushed becomingly. "Although I was hoping to learn more French recipes, Cook showed me some of her traditional English favorites—"

"Though I must admit Mlle. le Duc's technique for preparing *mille-feuille* is quite ingenious—"

"And then the oven started to heat in irregular patches—"

"Which Mlle. le Duc had not only seen before, but successfully resolved in her own kitchen with tongs and a chisel—"

"It's not a '*remède*,'" Désirée said quickly. "I mean, it *is* a *remède*, but it's not a '*grand*' *remède*, of the sort where—"

"I rescind the question," Jack interrupted.

The fact that glimpsing her disheveled with

a smudge of flour on her cheek and a hammer in her hand made him want to kiss her even more proved the desperate need to set clear and immediate boundaries.

He gave her a pointed stare. "Might we talk privately for a moment?"

She set down the hammer and nodded.

"My office, please."

He led her into his private study, seated her across from him in the guest chair, and steepled his fingers atop his desk in a manner he hoped projected the image of a man who had everything under control.

Inside, his head was spinning.

Désirée had been using her free time to apprentice "English recipes" in the Skeffington kitchen. Cook, for her part, had seen no objections to playing chef-master, nor to utilizing the family governess as a culinary handyman. And it had all turned out peaches.

Blast it all. Désirée's brain inflamed his passions just as potently as her beauty.

"No kissing," he blurted out.

She shook her head rapidly. "Cook and I were just… *cooking*."

"Not you and…" He stared at her. Blinked. Shoved the image out of his mind. "I meant you and me. I have no honorable intentions, except to my family. My children and their best interests will always come first."

She nodded. "That is what I like best about you. 'Family first.' I feel the same."

There. Splendid chat. Everything was resolved.

Except it wasn't. Only the thinnest sliver of self-control prevented him from bending over the desk and kissing her right then and there. Nothing would be resolved until they were both out of temptation's way.

"I need to find a permanent governess for my children."

Her brow furrowed in confusion.

Possibly because he'd just stated the original, already-agreed-upon plan, rather than announce some earth-shattering new development.

She tilted her head. "How is the hunt going?"

Horribly. Primarily because he hadn't been hunting.

"Confession." He cleared his throat. "I don't know *how* to find the sort of governess we need. If I knew, I wouldn't have come to you to start with."

"We can search together." She reached for one of the pencils in their receptacle. "May I?"

"Anything." He opened his top drawer and handed her a stack of fresh foolscap.

She sharpened the pencil with a knife she apparently kept on her person—he tried valiantly not to let this new detail bewitch him even more—and wrote *REAL GOVERNESS* on the top of the paper.

"Let's start at the beginning." She underlined the title twice. "What do you want?"

Someone to nurture, entertain, and educate his children.

Someone with a distant but foreseeable leaving date: when his twins turned seventeen.

Someone tolerable enough to join the family for several years, but not so essential that they would be devastated at her inevitable departure.

Someone kind, competent, and caring.

Someone he and his children definitely wouldn't fall in love with.

"Knowledgeable," he said at last. "Experienced."

Désirée added these items to the page. "Knowledgeable in which subjects, specifically? How many years' experience?"

Over the next quarter hour, they managed to flesh out a detailed profile, complete with expectations regarding education, rules, castigation, meals, schedules, free time, autonomy, milestones, salary, and more.

He leaned back. "Now what?"

"Now…" She tapped the edge of the pages

against the desk to align them. "We take out an advertisement in all the papers."

"An advert for what?" came a voice from the corridor.

Annie and Frederick stood in the doorway with sleep-lined faces and curious eyes.

"Your new governess," Jack informed them.

"Your *real* governess," Désirée corrected. "Someone who is practically perfect in every way."

Frederick sent narrowed eyes toward his father. "Someone who will make us do long division?"

Jack widened his eyes. "Relentlessly."

Annie crossed her arms. "I hate new people."

Frederick copied his sister's stance. "Me, too."

"You both adore new people," Jack reminded them. "You know everyone in town, and everything about every new tourist within minutes of their arrival."

"They're not governesses," Annie informed him. "They're *gossip*."

"You shouldn't gossip," Frederick whispered.

"You're just jealous because you aren't interesting enough to be gossiped about," Annie shot back.

Jack reached for the freshly organized papers. "Would you like to hear our list of re-quirements?"

"No," Annie said. "I despise her already."

Frederick elbowed her in the ribs. "What if it's Miss Quincy? She's not a stranger and she likes to play with us."

"It is not Miss Quincy." Jack cast a be-seeching gaze heavenward. "She married the Duke of Azureford. Governesses can't be married."

Annie wrinkled her nose. "Or what?"

"Or they go away," Frederick answered. "We don't want anybody who's going to go away."

"She'll go away when we're grown up," Annie reminded him.

Frederick shook his head. "Not if she likes us. She'll come over for tea from time to time, and we'll laugh about how we used to put pins on her chair and toads under her pillow."

Jack dropped his face into his hands.

Désirée rescued the list of requirements and added *PATIENCE* at the top in capital letters.

He nodded in agreement. This wasn't going to be easy.

CHAPTER 7

*O*ne week. Désirée had been interim governess for one week. After placing an advert the morning after she and Jack had almost kissed, they had been assiduously avoiding each other ever since out of self-preservation.

Keeping out of temptation's reach seemed the only sure way to stay out of each other's arms.

Yesterday was Sunday. Her first "free" day. She had spent every moment of it with her brothers in the hope that keeping Jack out of sight meant he would also stay out of mind.

It had not worked.

Today she was back to work. Breakfast at eight, lessons at nine. Unfortunately, it was half past six and she hadn't slept a single moment all night.

Out of pity for Hester, her borrowed lady's maid, Désirée had washed and dressed herself and brushed her own hair. Restless, she tiptoed out of her room and down the stairs to the garden door at the rear of the cottage. A brisk, restorative walk in the early autumn air would be just the thing.

A distant *whizzzzz...thunk* caught her attention. It almost sounded as though someone was shooting arrows just beyond the trees.

She crept forward to investigate who on earth would be out here practicing archery at dawn.

Who, it turned out, was Jack Skeffington. Despite the cool weather, his greatcoat was tossed carelessly atop a large rock, and his shirtsleeves billowed piratically in the wind.

He was not, however, practicing archery. An impressive pile of knives teetered atop a flat stone. One by one, he picked up each blade and hurled it across the stream to an evergreen opposite. A pile of spent knives grew at the foot of the trunk as each new throw knocked the previous blade from its perch.

She should leave. If the knives didn't scare her, Jack's taut, muscular, semi-undressed body definitely should. Yet her legs stepped forward rather than run away.

A twig snapped beneath her feet.

Jack turned, presumably startled, although the blade sailing from his fingers arced perfectly to the precise spot on the same tree as all the others.

"Did I wake you?" he asked.

Désirée shook her head. He could not wake her. Thoughts of him had prevented her from sleeping in the first place.

She stepped closer. "What are you doing?"

"Throwing knives." A slow, mischievous smile curved his lips. "Want to try?"

Her brothers would murder her.

"Yes. Absolutely." She hurried to his side, and stared doubtfully from the pile of sharp blades to the suddenly impossibly distant evergreen on the other side of the stream.

He handed her a knife, then demonstrated with his own. "Hold the handle like this. Relax your stance. Right foot forward, left behind. Straight spine. Mind the spin. If your knife falls in the water, you have to fetch it."

She swallowed. "Should I perhaps practice on a closer tree?"

"Distance first, accuracy second. It doesn't matter how straight your aim if your weapon cannot reach its mark."

"'Mark' meaning someone's chest?"

"'Tis better to aim for the eyes," he suggested helpfully. "The heart is stuck behind so many meddlesome ribs, your blade is as likely to glance harmlessly off the bone as pierce into a ventricle."

"'Harmlessly,'" she repeated. "We wouldn't want that."

"Shoulders back. Suck in your stomach. Mind your hips." He stepped behind her to help nudge her elbow and shoulders into place. "Think about your *power*. When the knife leaves your hand, keep throwing. Don't limit the momentum."

She hurled the knife with all her might.

The blade cleared the stream. Désirée stumbled forward. The knife knocked into the base of the wrong tree, handle first, several feet closer than the evergreen she'd meant to hit. A rush of excitement like no other flooded her veins.

She shoved a windblown hunk of hair out of her eyes and spun to face Jack, bouncing on her toes in excitement. "Can I try again?"

He grinned at her. "We have until breakfast."

"Show me again how to stand," she ordered.

He tucked a loose tendril behind her ear. "First, we need to keep your hair out of your eyes."

"Hester is still asleep," Désirée admitted. "That's why it's just in a knot. I am afraid I don't have a *'remède.'*"

"I do." He dipped his fingers into his waist-coat pocket and pulled out a dozen hair pins. "Turn around."

She blinked. "You carry around knives and hair pins?"

"Mmph." He clamped all but one in his teeth and motioned for her to get into position.

She turned around.

His fingers were as deft in matters of hair as they were deadly in the throwing of knives. He untwisted her knot in order to fashion it more tightly, his touch firm but gentle as he trapped all loose flyaways with an expertly placed pin.

"*Now* you're ready," he pronounced. Even the blustery autumn wind could not disrupt his handiwork. "Do you remember how to stand?"

"No," she said quickly. Too quickly. *Touch me again.*

The heat in his eyes indicated he saw right through her ruse, but he once again placed his strong, warm hands on her shoulders, her spine, her hips.

She almost forgot to breathe.

He stepped away. "Now throw."

She threw.

The blade still hit the wrong tree, but higher this time. The knife hit handle first again, but managed to dislodge a tiny bit of bark from the trunk.

Désirée felt like a knife-throwing *savante*.

"Is knife-wielding a trick your governess taught you?" she teased.

"Didn't have one," he answered. "Everything I know, I learned at my father's knee. That's probably why it's taken me so long to realize my children were ready for more. Now that the war's over, maybe they'll grow to be something other than privateers."

She had forgotten he'd once worked for the government. "Were you a 'legitimate' pirate for long?"

"I spent years storming shores and seas in the name of Crown and King. I even received a few souvenirs for my trouble." He touched the tip of a blade to the jagged scar on his cheek. "This one was actually courtesy of a land battle. Enemy soldiers can be tricky rascals."

A sick feeling pooled in her stomach. "French soldiers?"

"Dead soldiers," was all he would say as he launched his knife across the stream.

But he hadn't denied it.

"You must hate them," she said softly, her voice scratchy. *You must hate us.*

"It's wise not to let one's guard down with mercenaries who would like to kill you." He handed her a knife. "And it's foolish to judge an entire population based on one group or one leader."

"We are divided amongst ourselves," she admitted. "That is what started the revolution. The royalists believe God and primogeniture give them status over others. The peasants believe such systemic inequality to be a self-serving evil worth killing to stop."

Jack's frown deepened. "Which were you?"

"Most of my family met the wrong end of a guillotine." Her smile was brittle. "That was then. Napoleon Bonaparte granted most émigrés amnesty many years ago. We would have returned at once, if we had been old enough. Now Uncle Jasper is too old, and we will have to make the trip alone. But there is nothing for him there. He is not French."

Or a royalist went unsaid.

Jack tested the weight of a blade. "I see."

She was certain he did. Britain had much the same structure, but Jack did not gain from it. He had no title. Scarcely better than a peasant, by her parents' standards. Born to be lesser, no matter what he might achieve in life.

Many émigrés had trickled home. But only after the restoration of the Bourbon monarchy a few months ago, had their status and superiority been fully reinstated. Being heir to a title was no longer a death knell, but a return to wealth and popularity.

Their birthright, Lucien called it. The wellspring of Désirée's missing dowry.

Jack hurled his knife across the stream.

Désirée did not tell him she was not a royalist. She did not tell her brothers, either. It didn't matter. A prince inherited his kingdom regardless of whether he found the process *fair*.

She threw her knife after his. "Our scars are not visible, but the war left its mark on my family, too. We started with more and ended with nothing. Not even our parents."

Her father had not even been next in line for the title. Sixth, eighth, with an entire generation of strapping young lads between, all destined to marry well and birth many healthy heirs of their own.

Except they hadn't. Lucien was now perhaps second or third in line. And all three siblings would give it up in a heartbeat if it meant they could have their home back, and their loved ones, and their innocence.

But the past could never be undone.

Jack reached for another knife. There were none. They had thrown them all. So he reached for Désirée instead.

"I do not blame you for the actions of your

ancestors or countrymen." His hands lifted hers, but they did not pull her close.

She did that on her own. The wind was cold, and his arms were warm. Perhaps they were on opposite sides of a war, but that war was over. If it had taught her anything at all, it was that everything in life was transient, and she must take care to enjoy everything good that came her way while she still had it.

He seemed to be reaching a similar conclusion. His arms had not let her go.

"We should stop."

"Should we?" She tilted her face up toward his. "I did not think we had started."

"I'm not a gentleman," he warned her. "I'm... a smuggler."

"The same is true of my brothers," she reminded him. "Your collaborators."

His thumb rubbed the bare skin of her upper arms. The resulting gooseflesh had nothing to do with the crisp autumn breeze and everything to do with the hard, strong man before her.

He lowered his head closer to hers. "Stop me."

"I don't want to." She rose on her toes to meet him.

"This leads nowhere." The tip of his nose brushed hers. "I'm not looking for anything lasting."

"Neither am I," she whispered. Soon, she would be gone from his life for good. "Kiss me while you still can."

Their lips crushed together like the tide crashing ashore: beautiful, unstoppable, inevitable. Her hands gripped his shoulders to keep from drowning. Her heart pounded as she pressed closer, heedless of the current threatening to drag them ever deeper.

She knew it led nowhere. The tide came only to leave again, no matter the destruction its touch left behind. Even though his kiss felt like everything, she knew it was nothing. And yet all she wanted was more. To dive in, no matter how treacherous the water.

A memory was always a better choice than regret.

"Maybe they're over here!"

Panting, Désirée and Jack leapt apart from each other just as Annie and Frederick burst through the trees.

"Twenty minutes until breakfast," Annie sang out.

"Can we play hoops?" Frederick lifted a large iron ring in each hand. "All we need are trundling sticks."

Annie darted forward and grabbed a long stick from the underbrush. "Found mine!"

"Our tournament was last night," Frederick

reminded her. "I want to see how Papa and Désirée do."

"Mademoiselle le Duc," Jack corrected.

It was too late. Désirée was Désirée, and the twins were too busy tugging them out of the woods and toward the street to bother with social niceties.

"I hope you brought your handkerchief," she warned Frederick. "I could trundle hoops in my sleep. Tears are going to fall when you see me utterly destroy your father."

Annie squealed in delight. "I'm in Désirée's team!"

"There's no *teams*," Frederick scolded her. "There's two hoops. One against one."

"Yes, but when *she* wins, I win, too!"

"Thank you for the confidence," Jack said. "I'll have you know these aren't my first hoops, either."

"Oh?" Désirée's keen gaze quickly assessed the two rings before she selected the best one. "Tell us. How old were you when you smelted your first trundling hoop in the boiling maw of the family forge?"

"Er…" Jack pantomimed loosening his cravat. "Can I be on her team, too?"

Frederick cried tears of laughter. "Too late! Too late!"

"Come one, come all, it's a fight to the finish.

And the finish is…" Annie pointed down the winding road. "First to the dairy's fence wins!"

"Do you want my stick?" Frederick asked Désirée.

Jack's jaw dropped open. "Is *anyone* in my team?"

"On three," Annie shouted in glee. "One…"

Désirée tossed Frederick's stick to his father and scouted one of her own.

"Two…"

Jack positioned himself at the top of the hill.

Désirée strategically broke certain twigs from her branch and assumed her position on his other side.

"Three!"

Désirée raced down the side of the mountain. Subtle adjustments of her stick kept her well-balanced iron hoop smooth and upright with practiced dexterity.

Jack's slightly uneven hoop pitched this way and that at every dip or pebble, forcing him to parry and feint as though he were not trundling hoops but fencing aboard a pirate ship.

Désirée immediately slowed and twisted about to jog backward, not rushing ahead to put paid to the race, but instead making an exaggerated show of staying precisely one step ahead.

The children crowed with laughter.

"That's it," Jack growled. "I'm going to—"

But whatever he was going to do did not get done, because his hoop chose that exact moment to exert its independence from both Jack and his stick.

"Désirée!" Frederick cried. "Quick, do a *le duc!*"

He wanted a *'remède?'* She would show him one of her favorites.

Before Jack could rescue his hoop, Désirée swung her arm in a half circle, catching the runaway iron ring with the opposite side of her stick. Now her branch trundled both; a two-foot long oak axle with unhinged wheels.

It took significantly more effort to keep the misaligned hoop in synchronization with the better-weighted one, but these were far from the worst hoops Désirée had ever been forced to trundle. She had been her brothers' official toy-tester since their very first day at the smithy.

"The fence!" Annie yelled in delight. "You were first!"

Désirée's stick and the hoops flew in opposite directions as the children tackled her about the waist, jumping and embracing her as if they had won the Crown Jewels.

She hugged them back instinctively. Désirée had known the twins all their lives, but after spending entire days of nonstop time with them, she could not deny the truth: she'd fallen in love with these ten-year-old terrors. Walking away was going to be one of the hardest things she'd ever had to do.

Jack rescued the fallen hoops. "Let's try one more time. Best two out of three."

"You're right," Annie giggled. "That would only take one more time."

Jack scooped his daughter off of Désirée and tossed her over his shoulder, where he attacked her with tickles. "You dare wager against your own father? Do you, ungrateful little scamp? Do you?"

Frederick and Désirée fell in beside them, each carrying an iron hoop.

"Can you teach me that trick?" Frederick begged. "I'll beat *everyone*."

"As soon as you memorize your multiplication tables," she promised.

"Aww," Frederick groaned, but his eyes were shining, no doubt already plotting his victory dance.

When they reached the house, Jack deposited Annie at the breakfast table.

"Start without me." He gestured at his wrinkled sleeves. "I have to rescue my coat before the goldfinches turn it into a nest."

Annie and Frederick piled plumb cakes and sausage onto their plates and wolfed down half before Annie looked up and sent Désirée a wounded expression. "Do we *have* to have a different governess?"

Désirée's heart gave a twinge. "I am afraid so."

"I don't want a replacement." Frederick scowled at her.

"No one could take your place." Annie crossed her arms. "No one else can be you."

"That is not how it is. Watch this." Désirée reached across the table and pulled their breakfast plates out of reach.

"Bad form," Frederick protested. "I was eating that sausage!"

"You already ate one," she reminded him. "Where is it now?"

He narrowed his eyes. "In my stomach."

Désirée turned to Annie. "And yours?"

"In my stomach." She patted her belly to illustrate. "But there's another on my plate."

"You want to eat another sausage?"

Both twins nodded warily.

"Here." Désirée speared a fresh sausage with each child's fork and handed it back.

The meat disappeared in a blink.

"Where's the second sausage?" she asked Frederick.

His brow furrowed. "In my stomach."

"And the other sausage?" she asked Annie.

"Also in my stomach."

"So, the second sausage didn't 'replace' the first sausage?"

The twins shook their heads. "They're still in our bellies."

"That's right." Désirée circled around the table to crouch between them. "Now imagine people instead of pork, and your heart instead of your belly. You can fit as many people inside here—" She touched Frederick's chest. "—as you are brave enough to let in. Even if it means a new governess."

Annie's lip wobbled.

Desiree cupped her cheek. "Loving someone in the future doesn't mean you loved someone in the past any less. It means you were lucky enough to have had two fine sausages in your life instead of just one."

CHAPTER 8

*L*ater that evening, after reading to his children an hour earlier than usual, Jack instructed his kitchen to begin wassail preparations for that night's festivities, then headed to his study.

In the five days since taking out the advert, his wide mahogany desk nearly bowed from the tower of eager responses his listing had generated.

Jack had yet to open any of them.

His days had been too full of coordinating the constantly changing smuggling operations —punctuated by boisterous meals, competitive hoop trundling, and the occasional knife throwing lesson—to possibly have any spare time to devote to the governess search.

His children were going to miss Désirée. *He*

was going to miss Désirée. They worked so well together as a team. Almost like a family.

He tore open the wax seal on the first query in the pile. Very experienced governess. Impressive command of an endless list of subjects. A list of references that looked like a summary of regular patrons to Almack's.

She wouldn't do.

He opened the next one on the pile, and the next, and the next. Perhaps he had undersold the twins' rambunctiousness. Perhaps he had oversold the price he was willing to pay to the right person.

Every single solicitude had more extensive credentials and glowing references than the last.

He shoved the rest of the stack away unopened and rubbed his face with his hands.

Jack was used to things not being easy. He was used to putting in the work, trying as hard as he could for as long as necessary until he achieved whatever it was that he needed to do.

The governess hunt was the opposite sensation.

He had told Désirée he wasn't looking for an Oxford professor, but the truth was, Jack could afford one if he wished to. Hell, half the women in this pile seemed like they could offer an education to rival any university.

Not that his children *needed* fancy schooling.

The smuggling windfall wouldn't last forever, especially now that Boney had been sent to Elba and peace was on the horizon.

To compensate for an uncertain future, Jack had spent the past several years learning the art of investing through trial and error. So, *so* much error.

It was no longer a challenge, but a skill. His coffers now had enough of a cushion that if French brandy became legal tomorrow and his smuggling career ended overnight, neither he nor his children would ever have to worry about money.

He'd wanted his children to be educated not because they needed to find work, but because he wanted them to be intelligent. To have more opportunities, more choices, more freedom than he or his father or his father's father had ever had.

Now here he was, seated before a literal tower of educational possibilities, and all he could think was:

None of those women were Désirée.

He liked her. No, this was worse than mere liking. He was becoming attached to her. Starting to feel like she was not an addition to his life, but an intrinsic part of it. That when she left, things would not return to normal, but instead be left with a piece missing.

Incomplete. *Again.*

This was the agreement they had made, he reminded himself. He had warned her he wasn't looking for anything lasting, and she had warned him of the very same thing. She and her brothers would rather return to the place where their parents were beheaded than stay here in Cressmouth. He had to be respectful of that.

He ought to *support* it. If he had suffered a missing piece, the le Ducs had been forced to survive as the only pieces left. What could be lonelier than that? If Jack was a true friend, he could shave off an inconsequential sliver of his wealth and hand it to them to pay off their debts and finance the family's return journey home.

Not that any of the stubborn le Ducs would accept charity. Their pride would have them calling for dueling pistols at dawn rather than swallowing the implication that they required the aid of an English commoner.

The corner of Jack's mouth quirked. He ought to make the offer anyway, just to see the look on Lucien's face.

Bastien, on the other hand… Bastien was the more level-headed of the two brothers. The most pragmatic. Bastien would accept coin from the hands of his enemies if it helped him achieve his goals. He'd have the family aboard the next boat to France before sunrise, and Jack…

Jack would have only himself to blame for losing Désirée all the faster.

Distant pounding sounded on his front door. The carolers! He strode to Désirée's chamber to see if she was ready to go wassailing.

She was ready. Oh, was she ever ready.

Her hair was piled atop her head with little tendrils falling artfully from each side to invite his fingers to touch. Her half-dress of translucent pearl covered a shell of shimmering turquoise beneath. He longed to slide his hands betwixt the gauze and the satin, to pull her to him and cover her mouth with his.

Instead, he offered his elbow as was polite and escorted her into the front drawing room. From the bustle and noise, it appeared half the adult villagers had gathered to eradicate Jack's wine supply rather than to sing door-to-door.

Was it any wonder he loved this town?

When at last his neighbors were sufficiently tipsy from Jack's wassail, they trooped out the door and into the street en masse, in search of the night's first victims.

"Have you gone wassailing before?" he asked Désirée.

She shook her head. "I know everyone from other things."

They certainly knew her. Although the le Ducs tended to keep to themselves, they were one of the most infamous families in Cressmouth. Those with carriages had had this or that fixed at the smithy, but *everyone* had seen them race their nimble phaeton through the woods, over streams, up and down the main hill.

Might as well paint a French flag on the bonnet, the baker had once said. *Everyone knows that racer belongs to the le Ducs.*

Sour grapes, Jack presumed. To his knowledge, that phaeton had never been bested.

The group linked arms at doorstep after doorstep, belting out one slurred rendition of *The Twelve Days of Christmas* after another, in exchange for more wassail that they definitely did not need. It might only be September, but Christmas had definitely arrived in Cressmouth, and it was indeed the most wonderful time of the year.

Désirée shamelessly making up English-sounding syllables to the verses she didn't know —which appeared to be most of them—had Jack grinning at her most of the night instead of paying attention to his surroundings.

Someone else might have opted not to join

in the fun, he realized. Not Désirée. She accepted every challenge head on and played to win. Joyfully. This would go down in history as one of his friends' favorite caroling escapades yet.

When at last the caroling came to an end, Jack doubted he and Désirée needed any more wine, but he invited her into the cellar anyway. They left the bottles on their shelves and tumbled into the pair of plush chairs by the fire.

"Admit it," he said. "You'll miss singing drunkenly to songs you've never heard of when you return to France."

She giggled and gave a *Who, me?* shrug. "Sometimes my feelings about returning to France are very complicated. And my feelings on having conflicted feelings are just as complicated."

He lifted her hand in his. "How do you feel about Cressmouth?"

"I feel in conflict," she admitted. "It's complicated when you don't quite fit in anywhere."

"What are you talking about?" he asked in surprise. "You fit in *everywhere*. The jeweler was happy to see you, the dairy maid was happy to see you, the local reporter was happy to see you, the stud farmer was happy to see you, the—"

She shoved his shoulder to get him to stop.

"That is because everyone in Cressmouth is friendly. And maybe a little drunk."

"A wee bit," Jack conceded.

Certainly that explained why he was waxing maudlin over the reminder that Désirée wouldn't just stop being his children's governess—she'd cease being part of their lives altogether. She wasn't moving out of the village. She was leaving the country. For good.

"One kiss," he said as he pulled her out of her chair and onto his lap. "One kiss, and we both go upstairs to our separate bedchambers and definitely don't spend the rest of the night thinking about what might have happened if we hadn't cleaved to our extremely professional demarcation lines."

"Seems reasonable." She bit her lip. "One kiss."

It wasn't one kiss. It could never be. The moment his lips touched hers, his soul was lost, surrendering to the moment and the nectar of her kiss. She tasted like wassail and mischievousness, of Christmas carols and long winter nights. Her sweet embrace heated him more thoroughly than any parlor fire. He was aflame, and she his only cure.

He would have kissed her into midnight, into dawn, into next week, had that been an option available to them. He would never leave this cellar if it meant he also need not ever leave her arms. To kiss her was to surrender tiny pieces of his armor. If they did not stop soon, she would strip every defense away and reveal him for what he was:

A man who would give his entire kingdom for one more kiss.

CHAPTER 9

"*G*ood work today, you two." Désirée set down the slate and brushed off her hands. "You are now free to do as you please until supper time."

"Hoops!" Frederick burst out of his chair and ran out of the schoolroom. He had been practicing the two-hoop trundle at every opportunity, and very nearly had the trick of it.

Annie, however, did not move. She stared up at Désirée with curious eyes until she finally blurted out, "Why doesn't your pig have a French name? Is he really your uncle's pig?"

Sometimes Désirée was almost certain Annie put up with her just to secure more playtime with the le Duc family hog.

"Chef *is* a French name," she answered. "It can mean something like 'master cook,' as it does in English, but it also means 'leader' or

117

'manager' or 'director.' In his head, Chef really is in charge and we are *his* pets."

Annie giggled. "Can you teach me French?"

Désirée arched her brows in surprise. "Would you like to visit France one day?"

"*No.*" Annie wrinkled her nose. "But I would like to have a secret language with you. We can tease Frederick and he won't even know! It can be a *le duc* just for you and me to share. We can eat *mille-feuille* and whisper in French."

Désirée hid a smile. As far as secret languages went, French was perhaps not the best choice—Annie's father as well as several entire countries could speak it—but the idea that Annie saw Désirée's cultural differences as aspirational rather than objectionable warmed her heart.

"Very well," she said. "If you meet me here in the school room half an hour before breakfast every morning, I will teach you French."

"Thank you!" Annie leapt from her chair and flung her arms about Désirée in a quick squeeze. "I'm going to go find Frederick, but I'm not going to tell him anything!"

She shot out the door.

With a shake of her head, Désirée closed the school room door and went to the large sash windows in the front parlor. Out in the street, Annie and Frederick were arguing over the iron hoops. Désirée made a mental note to have her brothers create two perfect new ones for each twin, so they could both double-trundle at the same time.

She glanced at the clock upon the mantle. Soon, the kitchen would begin preparing tonight's meal. Although the offerings were relentlessly English, Désirée had taken to lending a hand more often than not in order to learn how to prepare a few new dishes.

When she returned home with new skills, her brothers might not be so impressed, but Uncle Jasper would appreciate the expanded menu.

On her way to the kitchen, light spilled into the corridor from the open door to Jack's study. He glanced up just in time to motion her to come in and join him.

"Finished for the day?" he asked as she sank into the chair opposite his desk.

"Annie and I have a secret," she said with a teasing smile.

He narrowed his eyes. "It better not be pins on my dining chair and toads under my pillow."

"I will never tell," she answered solemnly.

"I have a secret, too," he said. "Parenting is hard."

Désirée imagined *that* verdict was about as

proprietary as French as a secret language, but refrained from quibbling at minor details.

"Your children are splendid," she assured him. "Very clever and capable and confident."

"And very ten-years-old." He made a face. "My apologies. I have no place to fish for sympathy. When you were their age, your life was unimaginably harder."

Désirée did not have to imagine it. She had lived the horror. Losing everything and doing anything to stay alive amid constant terror. She would not wish it on anyone.

"My family was not the only one to experience tragedy. Yours did, too." She met his eyes. "Especially you."

He blinked at her as if she was the first to acknowledge that the loss of a wife was every bit as devastating and life-altering as his children's loss of their mother.

"I believed in love, and marriage that lasted forever," he said after a moment. "And then eight years into my marriage, it was all over. I divided my time between the nursery and the sickbed, but even without sleeping I could never do enough. But I tried. Husband and father. Nursemaid and lady's maid. Nanny and footman. It didn't matter."

"Of course it mattered," Désirée said softly. "Just because someone we love is now gone doesn't mean the time we shared with them was for naught."

She remembered meeting his wife. Sweet-tempered, moneyed, cultured. By all accounts, a "perfect English rose." Exactly the sort of woman any Englishman would boast to have on his arm. The opposite of Désirée in every way.

"All the same," Jack said. "I'm not going through that again."

"I don't blame you."

That was the danger of loving people. Sometimes, you weren't able to keep them.

Désirée's loss had been sudden. The death of Jack's wife had been prolonged and painful. She and her siblings had not been afforded the chance to say goodbye, or even to process what was happening. He and his children had been forced to watch a loved one suffer. Neither outcome was better.

The only way to protect one's heart was not to risk it in the first place.

"Afternoon post, sir." A footman appeared in the doorway.

Désirée was grateful for the interruption. Living in the past was not good for anyone. It was time to think about the present.

The footman lifted a tall stack of letters from a silver tray and placed them atop Jack's desk.

"You have got to be bamming me." Jack stared at the teetering pile, then back up at his footman. "We're still receiving responses to that advert?"

The footman lifted his chin. "I would never dare speculate on the contents of my master's correspondence."

"I am happy to speculate." Désirée pointed. "Those are definitely interested queries from potential candidates."

"How can there be this many unemployed, overqualified governesses in England?"

"Cressmouth is a popular destination and you offered a handsome wage," she pointed out. "Maybe they are not unemployed, but willing to switch allegiance for the right price."

"Cynical." Jack shoved the new pile next to the previous piles. "And no doubt correct."

"I can help sift through them," she offered. "Between the two of us, perhaps we can make short work of it."

She ignored the unwelcome pang in her stomach at the thought of helping him hurry along someone to replace her.

The footman lowered his silver tray toward Désirée. "For you, mademoiselle."

"For me?" Her surprise turned into a smile as she recognized Lucien's appalling penmanship. "Thank you."

She tore open the letter with eager fingers.

These infernal English books will be due in three days, and you promised you'd be home in time to return them.

She grinned. Although he did not confess it in so many words, Lucien had been studying just as he promised.

The pig misses you. Uncle Jasper says his snorts aren't quite the same.

Désirée missed her zany family, too. Seeing her brothers only once a week on her free day just made their absence all the sharper during the rest of the week.

I've recalculated the figures and I have good news! If the smithy stays as busy as it is now, we'll have the lease paid within six months. Just think—we'll be back home before spring!

Her heart gave a lurch. A fortnight ago, this would have been wonderful news, indeed. Summers in Brittany again. Winters in Bordeaux. France was the promised land, the gold at the end of the rainbow, their chance to start anew.

She hadn't expected her time with the Skeff-ingtons to feel like a second chance, too.

Désirée swallowed thickly. Just because any number of better qualified governesses could show up to replace her on the morrow, did not mean she must cut off all contact with Jack and his children. They would still be neighbors for a little while.

Hurry back so we can pack our valises for the final time...

"Everything all right?"

Désirée glanced up from the letter and nod-ded. "Nothing but good news."

Or so it should have been.

Her chest tightened. She wondered if six months would be enough time to teach Annie French before she left for good.

CHAPTER 10

*T*he following day, as soon as the children went outside to play, Jack invited Désirée to his private cellar for their now customary after-dinner glass of wine in the wingback chairs beside the fire.

At least, he continued to tell himself he was inviting her to a glass of wine. Certainly the cellar *contained* plenty of wine. If sometimes they forgot to drink it because their mouths were occupied with more pleasant activities, who could blame them?

The moment they took the final step into the cellar, he pulled her into his arms.

It was just kissing, he told himself as his mouth covered hers and his fingers sank deep into the silk of her hair. Kissing meant nothing more substantial than that they enjoyed each other's lips. Kissing wasn't promises. Kissing was passion. Simple and uncomplicated.

He loved the voluptuous feel of her soft body pressed against his. How perfectly they fit together. How every kiss demanded another. Knowing he would soon no longer have her should have sent him running away, but instead made him want to cuddle her even closer.

She should fear the same. The last thing she needed before returning to France was an entanglement with a father of two who couldn't leave Cressmouth. And yet her hands were locked tight about his neck, her tongue just as demanding as his.

He couldn't give her France and he couldn't offer forever, but they had *right here* and *for now* and *just kisses*.

So what if it wasn't enough? He could ignore that his longtime hobby of designing an imaginary farm in his head had turned into mental Désirée-ville instead. Instead of planting grapes, he was imagining picnics and hoop trundling and flower gardens and knife throwing and lazy nights on the sofa in the wine cellar with nothing between their bodies but the occasional flicker of firelight.

Dangerous is what thoughts like that were. He had to put a stop to it at once.

He wrenched his mouth from hers and deposited her in a chair before falling heavily into the matching chair at her side.

"So." He lifted his fist to his mouth and cleared his throat. "We were going to look through the latest solicitudes."

She nodded and fumbled for the top stack of queries piled between their chairs. "They're still here."

Of course they were. The plan had been to toss the letters of any obviously unsuitable candidates directly into the fire. This had resulted in the ashes of approximately two queries. Never let it be said that the many experienced governesses of England were unqualified for their posts.

While Désirée sorted today's pile of possibilities, Jack opened a Bordeaux merlot and poured her a glass.

"What are all these new stacks?"

"They are all good candidates," she explained, "so I am sorting by greatness. Years of experience from left to right, depth of subject matter from top to bottom."

"What about number of references?"

"Well, that's thorny." Her brow furrowed. "If a marvelous governess has been with a large group of siblings since birth, she conceivably only has the one reference. Whereas a middling governess who never keeps a post for more than few years at a time might have a dozen family names in her list."

"Fair point."

They slid from their chairs to the plush carpet to have better access to the growing array of governess profiles.

Désirée pointed. "That quadrant contains the least knowledge with the least experience. Keep in mind, that judgment is by comparison. They all seem like competent, upstanding ladies."

Jack nodded. "Into the fire."

He flung each folded paper into the flames as though he was skipping rocks by the bed of the stream.

She pointed again. "This quadrant contains highly experienced governess with a slightly lower breadth of knowledge." She moved her finger. "And that quadrant contains some of the cleverest women in the entire country, although they have marginally less experience teaching that knowledge to children."

"Burn them all," he pronounced cheerfully, and tossed both groups into the fire. "What now?"

"Now…" She picked up the remaining stack and began dividing it into four piles. "We keep trimming using requirements of diminishing essentialness until only one winner remains.

These women are all genius child-wrestlers, so I am dividing them by years in the same household along one axis, and sense of playfulness along the other."

Jack was beginning to think that instead of having Désirée sort through the post, he should have asked her to overhaul his entire smuggling empire.

He slanted her an assessing look. "I believe the cleverest woman in England might be sitting right here on my carpet."

"I won't be in England for long," she reminded him, and lifted a hand to hide her yawn. "These are the new divisions. Joyless butterflies in that quadrant—"

"Fire," Jack said and tossed them in.

"This one is joy*ful* butterflies and that one is joyless barnacles—"

"Fire and fire."

"And this one..." She yawned again and blushed. "My apologies. It has been a long day."

"Get some sleep." He touched her cheek. "I can sort through the joyful barnacles on my own."

She smiled into his palm. "There are no bad decisions. If you want your children to have the very best, literally any governess in that stack more than meets the criteria."

But as she disappeared up the staircase, he

couldn't help but wonder whether any of the ladies in the remaining *practically perfect* stack were truly who his family needed.

Rather than continue with the search, Jack corked the wine and snuffed the fire, and headed upstairs to his study.

Désirée didn't want to stay. He couldn't make her, and shouldn't try.

Instead, just as she was doing her utmost to ensure the best possible future for him and his family, Jack should do the same for her and hers.

Years ago, he and the le Duc brothers had reached a gentlemen's agreement as to what minor percentage of his income they would earn as a commission. Because a business like smuggling necessitated keeping paper evidence to a minimum, they simply had to trust Jack's word that he was passing along their fair share.

He had never shorted them so much as a penny. As his income grew, so did his payouts. The le Ducs knew he had just expanded into champagne, but as yet did not know what relative commission to expect.

Jack would make one up.

If they thought they were a year away from repaying their lease, Jack would ensure they received the equivalent to an annual sum by the end of the month. Why not? They needed the money, and he could afford the loss.

Of coin, anyway. When it came time to say goodbye to Désirée…

It didn't matter how *he* felt, he reminded himself. He was fortunate enough to have an entire stack of practically perfect governesses to choose from. His children would be fine.

He affixed a wax seal to his instructions to increase a certain monthly bank deposit, then startled to catch sight of the time. He was late to story time.

Quickly, he made his way to his children's bedchamber and settled himself in his usual spot between them on the bed.

"Tonight what chapter are you going to pretend you didn't sneak ahead to read?"

Annie thunked Gulliver's Travels to Jack's chest. "We definitely, probably, possibly, might not have read Part IV."

"Excellent." He opened the book. "That's exactly where I left off."

"Why were you late?" Frederick asked.

Rather than launch into an explanation of smuggling commissions, Jack simply said, "I've been sorting through the governess queries to find the perfect one for you two."

Annie and Frederick exchanged a look.

Jack put down the book. "What?"

"Shouldn't *we* get to pick what sort of governess we might like?" Annie asked.

"You," Jack replied, "are ten years old. As lovely as it might sound, I cannot allow you to choose a governess based on her propensity to hand out lemon drops and sleep past noon."

"We can be reasonable," Frederick protested. "We're not *babies*."

"And we don't wish to be ignorant," Annie added. "In fact, Désirée has been teaching me…"

"What?" her brother demanded. "Something without me? What is she teaching you? I want to know, too!"

"All right," Jack interrupted. "I can see you're both passionate about your education. I shall take all special requests into consideration."

Annie narrowed her eyes. "You will?"

"I promise." He set down the book to give them his full attention. "According to the world's most demanding ten-year-olds, what characteristics constitute the perfect governess?"

"Clever," Annie said at once.

"Fun," Frederick added immediately.

"Cheerful."

"Witty."

"Imaginative."

"Fearless."

"*French*," Annie said firmly.

"Good at hoops," Frederick added.

"Good at horse-riding," Annie countered.

"Good at everything."

Annie rubbed her belly. "Especially *mille-feuille.*"

"And '*remèdes.*'"

"With…" Annie stared at her brother helplessly. "…brown hair."

Frederick shook his head. "Mm, more of a biscuit color."

"Definitely biscuit-colored hair," Annie agreed. "Kind of not-quite-burnt biscuits."

"But brown eyes."

Annie held up a finger. "Good hugs."

"*Wonderful* hugs," Frederick corrected.

"And not afraid of frogs," Annie finished.

Both twins looked at him expectantly.

Jack understood the message.

"That is a tall order," he said slowly. "What if I found a governess like that, but she had other plans?"

Annie gripped his hand. "You'd have to convince her to stay."

Frederick nodded. "Convince her we're a *family.* Families stay together."

"What if that's the reason she can't stay? Because she already has a family who's going somewhere else, and they also think families should stay together?"

Annie's lip trembled. "Then... then life isn't *fair.*"

Jack's heart clenched in sympathy.

His children's temporary governess had perhaps taught them the hardest lesson of all.

CHAPTER 11

*T*wo days later at the supper table, Désirée was surprised when the first course was a traditional French favorite.

When the second course turned out to be a staple of the Aquitaine region, her surprise narrowed into suspicion.

"Is it Christmas?"

Annie wiggled in her seat. "We have a new chef! A *chef*-chef!"

"A *French* chef?" Désirée asked in disbelief.

Frederick's head bounced in obvious excitement. "Does it feel like home?"

She spun to face Jack. "You replaced *Cook?*"

"I did not replace Cook." He served himself an extra helping. "Our kitchen now boasts a Cook and a Chef. English and French, living in harmony."

"Mostly harmony," Frederick murmured. "Chef yells a lot."

"So does Cook," Annie whispered back.

"But why?" Désirée stammered. "Not the yelling—the cohabitation?"

"I remembered what you said," Jack replied. "About wishing you knew how to cook more French meals. Feel free to pester our new Chef as much as you like."

"Désirée doesn't 'pester,'" Annie defended staunchly.

Frederick wrinkled his nose. "Chef will definitely think it's a 'pester.'"

"Not if she pesters in *French*," Annie shot back.

Désirée shook her head in incredulity. "It *is* Christmas year-round here. This is a lovely development. Thank you."

It was all she could do not to dash immediately to the kitchen and present herself to the new chef.

Jack's eyes crinkled smugly. "We're glad you're pleased."

She *was* pleased. And a little confused. It was an extremely thoughtful gesture, as well as a way for her to more quickly prepare for re-assimilation into her ancestral home. It made her feel both valued and dispensable at the same time.

An odd sensation, now that her "few days" as interim governess had stretched nearly a month. There was no shortage of better qualified prospects to choose from. Perhaps this was a farewell present, meant to sweeten the goodbye.

"Tonight's the star walk," Annie said. "Don't forget."

Frederick huffed. "You used to want to go by yourself."

"Now we're going to go as a *family*." She glared at her brother. "All right?"

"All right," he muttered. "We're the Skeffington constellation. We go everywhere together."

Annie brightened. "Tell that to Mrs. Pringle during the first part of the tour. She loves fictional constellations."

"Eat," Jack commanded. "Or we'll miss the tour altogether."

They ate.

Désirée pretended she could not also see them kicking each other beneath the table.

Although she had lived in Cressmouth for many years, she had never participated in the monthly "star walk." Gloria Pringle, one of the area's most talented astronomers, had been giving the famed celestial tours about the castle grounds for more than a decade.

According to Jack, Annie had not missed a

single monthly tour since her first experience four years ago.

"Do you think you might like to be an astronomer someday?" Désirée asked her.

"I would if I could have an orrery. Mrs. Pringle has an orrery." Annie turned to her father. "Can I have a mechanical solar system?"

"No." He pointed to her plate. "Eat your snails."

"*Escargot*," she corrected sweetly, then winked at Désirée. "And that was the *apéritif*."

It was hard not to snicker.

"I want to be famous someday," Frederick announced.

Jack arched his brows. "Famous for doing what?"

Frederick frowned. "I haven't decided yet."

"Famous for being the slowest eater in the world." Annie stole *asperges mauves* from her brother's plate. "Make haste, or we'll be late."

"You know all the stars already," Frederick grumbled. "And the first half of the tour is make-believe."

But before long, they were bundled in hats and coats and scarves, and heading outside into the chilly night air.

"Where are the geese?" Annie cried when they came to the edge of the stream.

"It's cold," Jack said gently. "Perhaps they've migrated to—"

"There!" Frederick pointed up ahead at six white geese, crouched beneath an enclave of bushes in sight of the water.

Désirée squinted her eyes. "What are they doing?"

"Laying eggs," Annie squealed, clasping her mittens together and spinning around. "They're going to have a bigger family, too!"

Désirée shot a quizzical glance at Jack.

He lifted a shoulder and herded his children forward. "Come along. Nobody likes to be stared at when they're trying to lay an egg."

As they stepped from the private Skeffington property into the castle's public park, a couple Désirée did not recognize smiled at them as they crossed paths.

"Happy Christmas!" they sang out.

Tourists, then, enticed to Cressmouth by the promise of eternal Yuletide.

"Happy Christmas," Jack and his children cheerfully chorused back.

The couple looked expectantly at Désirée.

Very well. She would play along. "Happy Christmas."

"Ooh," cooed the woman. "How exotic. Where are you from?"

Désirée clenched her teeth. No matter how hard she tried, something about her *R*s never failed to give her away.

"Scotland," Annie replied before Désirée could answer. "We're Highlanders."

The woman blinked in confusion as her husband hurried along down the path.

"It's not nice to lie to strangers," Jack chastised his daughter quietly.

Annie looped her arm through Désirée's and lifted her chin in defiance. "It's not nice to make people feel like they don't belong. Especially when *they're* the ones who are outsiders and we're the ones who live here."

Désirée did not have the heart to tell her that tourists weren't the only ones who repeatedly brought her family's differences to their attention as if they were flaws.

She suspected it was the real reason Lucien did not wish to improve his English. Her brother preferred *not* to understand the judgmental comments well-meaning good people made right to his face. *Must they talk like that? Look like that? Eat like that? Live like that?* One tired of smiling vacantly and pretending not to comprehend the question.

She and her brothers were anomalies here. They could see they did not fit in. That was one of the many attractions to going back to France.

Nonetheless, Désirée loved Cressmouth. She knew it was the antithesis to southern France and felt like a bad le Duc for letting a wintry English village burrow its way into her heart, but the truth was she would miss this wonderful, maddening hamlet the moment she didn't have it anymore.

"We're here!" Annie raced out of the park to the foot of the castle steps, where a group of star-gazers was already forming.

Désirée made a mental note to run up to the lending library after they finished in order to send a new batch of books back home to Lucien. Perhaps even one on constellations.

Gloria Pringle grinned at them. "Just in time! Annie, would you like to be my apprentice tour guide today?"

"Annie is the apprentice tour guide every time," Frederick whispered to Désirée, "but the tourists don't know and think she's a darling."

Annie *was* a darling. So was her brother. Désirée gave his hand a quick squeeze and hid a smile when he let her.

She was glad the hunt for a real governess was taking inordinately long. If all she had left in Cressmouth were six short months, she'd happily spend them with the twins... and their father.

She glanced at Jack. She loved the way the

dark hair at the base of his neck curled against his starched cravat. His wide shoulders encased in perfectly tailored grey superfine. His tight-fitting buckskins, so touchably soft. His mouth, just as irresistible when smiling wickedly as when kissing her senseless. It was hard to pay attention to mere stars when he was in her sights.

Gloria pointed up at the sky. "See that constellation? What do you suppose it is? Use your imaginations."

Frederick rolled his eyes. "This is Annie's favorite part."

"A duke!" shouted one of the younger boys. "You've been wishing upon a duke ever since you were a baby!"

"That's Nigel," Frederick whispered. "He wants to be apprentice tour guide, but he's only seven. He memorized the pretend constellations."

"I don't need to wish upon stars anymore," Annie announced. "The Skeffingtons have our own duke, and she's standing right next to us."

Désirée jerked in alarm and took a step back. "Er…"

As she was neither a duke nor the property of the Skeffingtons, she did not know the right response.

She settled for a belated, "I… am not a duke."

"Of course you are." Gloria chuckled with good cheer. "Your family is one quarter of the local legend!"

Désirée blinked. "We're... part of the local legend?"

"An enormous part," Gloria confirmed, and turned to the crowd. "How many dukes do we have here in Christmas?"

"Twelve!" the crowd chorused.

"That's right. The legendary Twelve Dukes of Christmas include the Duke of Silkridge..." Gloria began.

"The Duke of Azureford," someone added.

"The Duke of Nottingvale," someone else yelled.

"*Désirée* le Duc," Annie called out.

"Sébastien le Duc," Frederick shouted.

Jack's merry eyes met hers. "Lucien le Duc."

"But... we..." Désirée tried to find words. "If I'm a duke, anybody can be a duke."

"Huzzah! Papa is also a duke." Annie curtsied to Jack. "How do you do, Your Grace?"

"Don't be silly, Annie," Gloria said with a straight face. "It isn't the Legend of the Baker's Dozen."

"You're still a duke to me," Annie stage-whispered to her father. "Even if you're extra. Your Grace."

Frederick looped his arm through Désirée's

and held on tight. "See? You can't leave. We'd end up with only nine Dukes of Christmas."

"Ten," Annie whispered. "I knighted Papa a duke."

"That's not how it works," Frederick snapped.

"If a constellation can be a duke, Papa can be a duke," she hissed back.

Jack touched Désirée's free elbow. "Is this arm spoken for?"

She shook her head in bemusement.

He placed her fingers in the crook of his elbow. "Your family might feel like outsiders because you came here eighteen years ago, but fifty years ago nothing was here on this mountaintop at all except a creaky abandoned castle. Mr. Marlowe created Christmas out of thousands of outsiders."

Her heart pounded. "I thought I was a misfit toy."

"We all are." He gave her a crooked grin. "That's what makes us family."

Annie tugged Désirée's scarf. "It's like having a whole *town* of breakfast sausages in your heart."

Jack stared at her. "*What?*"

Désirée burst out laughing. "Wise words, indeed."

She'd kiss all three of her favorite sausages if an entire tour group of witnesses weren't watching.

CHAPTER 12

*D*ésirée and Jack were ensconced in their usual evening nook in the wine cellar when a footman knocked on the staircase wall, just out of sight.

"Pardon the interruption, sir. A message has arrived."

"Come in, Hawkins."

Désirée watched Jack's face carefully as he accepted the missive from the footman. Although they had only been enjoying post-supper wine together for just over a month, this was the first time they had been interrupted. Something must be amiss.

A muscle worked in Jack's jaw as he read, then folded the letter. "I'll have to send a reply at once."

"His man is waiting at the door, sir, in the hopes of just that."

Jack glanced at the clock in the corner and winced. "Blast. I don't know how long this will take, and the twins are expecting their bedtime story. Désirée, can you handle it just for tonight?"

Could she take their father's place, unexpected and uninvited, to perform their father's beloved nightly ritual in what was now often the only time the twins enjoyed privately with their father all day?

No. She could not. It was not Désirée they wanted.

"Thank you," Jack continued without waiting for a reply, and tore up the stairs with his footman trailing close behind.

She rolled back her shoulders and trudged upstairs to disappoint the children.

"Why are you here?" Annie asked when Désirée walked into the room.

"To... read your bedtime story. If you would like me to."

Frederick narrowed his eyes. "Where's Papa?"

"He was called to his office to deal with important business." She took a deep breath. "He is very sorry he cannot read to you tonight. I know it is your special time with him."

The twins scooted away from each other in the bed.

"You're practically Papa," Frederick said.

Annie patted the blank space between them. "Papa always reads lying in the middle."

Désirée's eyes stung and her heart seemed too big for her chest. "I… Shouldn't I fetch the book first?"

The twins exchanged another glance.

"We might've already been reading it," Frederick admitted.

Annie nodded. "We might've actually finished it and started on a different book."

They each pulled a volume out from under their pillow.

"You can read from whichever one you like best," Annie added helpfully.

Désirée let out a shaky breath she hadn't realized she'd been holding and climbed up into the middle of the bed between the two children.

"Why all the subterfuge?"

Annie made a face. "Papa might stop reading to us if he realizes we can do it faster on our own."

"He knows," Frederick said darkly.

"I know he knows," Annie hissed. "But as long as we all pretend nobody knows, things will go on like they always have."

"But I am here," Désirée pointed out. "That is very different."

Frederick frowned. "Yes, but we *like* having you here."

"Perhaps your father also likes reading to you." Désirée touched his cheek. "Whether you're better at it without him or not. Maybe he comes here because he wants to."

Annie snuggled into Désirée's shoulder. "I wish you would *stay* because you want to."

"Not in bed," Frederick added. "In our family. We made room for you in our hearts, just like you said."

Annie gazed up at her. "Do you think you could make room in your heart for us, too?"

Throat stinging, Désirée hugged them both tightly. "You burst into my heart the day that I met you. Sometimes I think loving you two rapscallions takes up all the room I have inside."

They squeezed her back. "Us, too."

Désirée opened the book to mask her tumult inside. She had answered one of their questions, but not the other.

They were clever children. They would realize it meant that although she loved them very much, although their perfectly imperfect family tempted her like no other, she could not stay.

Not as a governess. Not with an end date from the first moment, knowing they would eventually no longer need her, and she'd be sent out the door.

As much as she yearned to prolong her stay, Désirée would go where she *was* needed. Bastien and Lucien loved her, too. Her family needed her not just for a few years, but for forever. They didn't have to make room for her. She already belonged with them.

After the twins were tucked into bed, Désirée returned downstairs to the wine cellar.

Jack was not there. She ignored the abandoned glasses of wine and instead curled up on the chair closest to the fire.

Not that she was cold. The children had warmed her heart. But she had told them a half-truth. The twins were not the only ones who had carved a place for themselves inside her chest. Her heart had grown big enough for Jack, too. *Missing* him was not nearly strong enough a word to describe how she would feel when she left.

Her gaze sank to the pile of governess queries on the carpet. These were the final contenders. The best of the best.

Part of her wanted to throw all six into the fire. And part of her wanted to grab one at random and beg her to start tomorrow, in order to put paid to the anguish of not knowing when the end would come.

Footsteps clattered down the stairs.

"Forgive me." Jack was in shirtsleeves. He

shoved a curl of tousled hair from his eyes. "There's an issue with one of the harbors. I've sent for my best man so we can find a solution, but... Why am I boring you with work? We haven't finished our wine." He collapsed onto the chair beside her. "How were the children? Are they still pretending they haven't finished *Gulliver's Travels*?"

She grinned. "Not with me. We're on to the next book. I hope you like pirates."

"Ghastly heathens, pirates." He shuddered theatrically. "Now, *smuggling*. That's a gentleman's profession."

Désirée placed her hands on her hips. "Aren't you going to ask if the twins were upset to have an unexpected substitute?"

"Bah." His eyes drifted closed. "You're a good mother. Of course they weren't upset."

Her heart flipped and her breath caught.

"You mean... I would *make* a good mother?" she ventured. "Someday?"

His eyes flew open. "Er... yes. That's what I meant. Obviously you're not their mother."

She nodded. "Obviously."

All sleepiness was gone from his face. His dark eyes held her immobile. "Désirée..."

"Don't say it."

Whatever *it* was. That she was a lovely person, *but*. That her interim must come to an end.

That she would never be more than a temporary substitute.

He touched her cheek. "I want you to know—"

She kissed him to shut him up.

She might be temporary, but she was not a substitute. She was *Désirée*. A woman with her own mind, and emotions, and desires. Soon she would be gone, but he would remember her. The *new* one would be the substitute.

He pulled her into his lap as though he could not stand for her to be even an arm's width away.

She felt the same. His body was so hard, his skin so hot. She ran her eager palms over his wide shoulders, his muscled arms.

"My jacket," he murmured against her lips. "I left it upstairs."

She tossed his cravat over the back of the chair.

His kisses deepened. "This is a dangerous game."

It was not a game.

She loved him, damn his hide, and she was going to leave him. He would hire a better governess and she would move to France.

But they had not done so yet. Her trunk was still upstairs, and the pile of queries was still on the floor unanswered. Until that changed, there was still time to take advantage of every moment they could, while they still had each other's arms to tumble into.

"I might be temporary," she murmured between kisses, "but I am here now. What are you going to do about it?"

His voice was husky. "What would you like me to do?"

"Everything."

He lifted her in his arms and deposited her on the sofa instead. He climbed atop her, propping himself up on one elbow to gaze down into her face.

"*Everything*-everything?" he asked again.

She reached for him. "Everything."

Love was not something she meant to curtail. Later, when they were separated by land and sea, what she would regret most would be any failure to take advantage of what little time they had together.

Not that she would admit this interlude to her brothers. Marrying off their virgin sister to some title enamored with the size of her governmentally reimposed holdings was their dream, not hers. She would rather die a spinster who had once given herself to love.

She tugged his shirt free from his waistband. He reached beneath her skirts and made her forget what she was doing altogether. His teeth lowered her bodice until her erect nipples appeared in the firelight. Her head lolled back as he suckled her breast and teased between her legs with his fingers until she was slick and feverish and panting.

"I want…" she gasped.

"We will," he promised. "But first…"

His fingers did something more, plunging and teasing, rubbing exactly where she most needed until her body spasmed with ecstasy.

Only then did he fling his shirt over his head and allow her access to his naked skin, as though he would permit himself no gratification until he was certain he had satisfied her first.

He had done so beyond reckoning. Her heart was still pounding and her limbs still boneless and spent. But the spot at her apex, the spot he'd coaxed into pure bliss, already throbbed with anticipation at the new pleasures yet to come.

She sank her fingers into his hair and pulled his mouth to hers. Next time wouldn't just be for her. Now they would find the peak together.

He fumbled at his waist, then fitted his hips to hers. His hands were embracing her, caressing her, and the thick heat jutting against her legs was something new. She wiggled against him, but he did not immediately penetrate.

"Not yet," he murmured. "You'll know when."

His shaft slid against her from the outside as he teased her breasts and nipples with his hands and mouth, stoking her just as expertly as he had done with his fingers.

When she thought she would die if he did not grant her release once more, only then did he position the tip of his shaft at the edge of where she wanted him most.

Still he hesitated, his gaze tortured.

"Désirée." The tip of his shaft barely nudged inside. "I can't promise…"

"Neither can I," she begged.

His gaze locked on hers. "But you still…"

"*Yes*." She tilted her hips upward, guiding him into her body.

His kisses swallowed her brief gasp of pain and then they were moving as one, giving, receiving, offering, taking. He waited until he had once again brought her to her peak before jerking free and clutching his fallen shirt to his loins.

He did not straighten their ruffled clothes, but instead pulled her into his warm embrace and held her close, his heart thundering just as fast as hers.

CHAPTER 13

*J*ack wasn't certain what to expect the following morning when the call of breakfast forced him and Désirée to face each other in the light of day.

Everything was unsettlingly normal.

Frederick was in raptures over new iron hoops the le Duc brothers had made for him.

Annie insisted on calling her tea *le thé* and her toast *le pain beurré*.

Désirée smiled at him from behind her teacup and motioned to a small ceramic tureen on the table next to the honey.

"Fresh blackberry *confiture*. Take your portion before it's gone."

She was acting exactly the same.

He had tossed her onto a sofa in his cellar, helped himself to her virginity, fallen asleep drooling on her shoulder… and she acted like nothing had changed.

Maybe nothing *had* changed. Wasn't that the agreement they'd struck? No expectations, no demands. No promises for the future, just like they both wanted.

At least, he was pretty sure that's what he wanted.

Kind of.

"Someone's here!" Annie pointed out the window.

They all turned in time to see a large black carriage teeter up. A grizzled man in a gold-spangled waistcoat leapt to the ground.

"Redmire." Here to solve their smuggling woes. Jack jumped to his feet just as his business associate stomped through the door. "If you'll excuse us."

"Got to get a new wheel," Redmire growled as he surrendered his hat and greatcoat to a footman. "Something's wrong with that carriage."

"Not your wheel," Désirée said politely as she smeared blackberry jam onto pound cake. "Rear axle, clear as day. I can have it mended for you within the hour."

Redmire looked at Désirée, swung his startled gaze to Jack, then swung his gaze back to Désirée. "Er… feel free to do that."

"But not until after breakfast," Annie called out. "We have blackberry jam."

Jack dragged Redmire into his study before the visit deteriorated further.

"What's the latest news?"

"Have to change harbors." Redmire spread a map out on Jack's desk. "This one. We haven't used it before. Be best if you came with me to scout it with your own eyes before we end up in the same scrape as before. You see things no one else can."

Jack hesitated. "I don't know if now is the right time."

"Of course it's the right time. If we don't go now, there's no more champagne." Redmire leaned back. "What's wrong with you? You've never acted namby-pamby about reconnaissance before."

Jack sighed. Redmire was right. Unless they found a safe, reliable route, their champagne dreams were over. "Let me just ask Désirée first."

Redmire stared at him. "Who the bloody hell is Désirée?"

"My… er…" Jack coughed into his hand. "That is, the twins' governess."

"You need to request smuggling permission from your brats' *governess?*" Redmire's splutter turned into sudden understanding. "Not the chit outside fixing my carriage?"

"She probably sent a note to her brothers," Jack muttered. "But, yes. That's the one."

"That *is* The One!" Redmire clapped Jack too hard on the back and roared with laughter. "I told you to find a good woman and you wasted no time at all. That's my Jack, king of efficiency. But why the devil is she still your governess if you really want her as your wife?"

"Wife?" Jack stammered faintly. "No, we... I didn't... She doesn't..."

"You haven't *asked* her?" Redmire spluttered. "What are you waiting for? Do you want me to go and do it?"

"*No*." Jack slapped his hands atop the map. "Do not propose to my children's governess on my behalf."

Redmire fished a cheroot from his waistcoat. "Are you happy?"

Jack nodded. "Yes."

"Your life better with her as part of it?"

"Yes."

Redmire narrowed his eyes. "You love her?"

Jack laughed. "Oh, come on. You know I'm not going through that again. Once was more than enough. I'm not foolish enough to..."

Redmire smirked at him knowingly.

Jack slumped into his chair. *Damn* it. He was in love.

"I swore I wouldn't do this," he muttered into his hands.

"You can't help it." Redmire chewed on his cheroot. "You're a pirate at heart. You find treasure, you want to hold it close. Marriage is just like smuggling."

Jack glared at him. "Marriage is not like smuggling."

"Marriage is *exactly* like smuggling. Have to be willing to lose later in order to win now. No risk, no reward. If you don't go after her while you've got the chance…" Redmire shrugged. "Going to be just like our access to Clicquot champagne. Gone forever."

"I can sort out the champagne," Jack said quickly. "Let me see that map."

Redmire pushed it forward without further comment.

Jack tried to make sense of the lines and squiggles, but all he could think about was his vow to never again risk his heart.

He knew what love was. He'd been there before. Which was how he knew Redmire was right—he'd fallen in love again. The second time was just as real. Just as dangerous. He'd never been more terrified. There were no more walls he could put up between him and Désirée because it was far too late. She was already inside.

Redmire tapped the edge of the map. "You want me to turn this right-side-up? Or…"

"I'm working on it," Jack snapped and spun the map around.

Now it was upside down.

"You pillock." He fixed the map and started tracing alternate routes with his finger.

He hadn't just fallen in love. He'd fallen in love with someone who intended to leave him forever. His hands went clammy. Jack couldn't let that happen. He *had* to find a way to un-temporary their arrangement. Not just for a few years, but forever.

Marriage. He'd never thought he'd consider the idea again.

He didn't even know if *Désirée* would consider it. Certainly her brothers would never allow marriage to an Englishman. Even one who preferred French wine.

Their plans for their sister were much loftier. They were aristocrats, for god's sake. Or had been, before the revolution. Perhaps could be, again. All they had to do was get their sister back home and out of Jack's clutches and then next thing you knew, she'd be *comtesse* this, or *marquise* that.

Jack couldn't offer her anything of the sort.

"I have an idea," Redmire said. "Why don't I scout the harbor and you secure the governess. I'll send you letters. With little hearts on them, since I know hearts scare you."

Jack leaned back to rub his temples. Redmire was right. Jack used to sail off at the drop of a hat, first as a privateer and then as a private investor. Wasn't love worth just as much risk?

For so long, he'd been a single father doing it all on his own. Smuggling brandy. Raising children. From the moment Désirée moved in, everything had changed for the better.

He could employ a new governess at the drop of a hat—the best governess in all of England, thanks to her—but no one could replace *Désirée*. He would have to overcome his fear of repeating the past if he hoped for a second chance for the future.

"All right." Jack shoved the map back toward Redmire. "Send me letters with little hearts and try not to get killed. Double your cut. I'll wrap things up on my end, one way or the other."

"See that you do." Redmire lit his cheroot.

Jack led him back to the dining room.

Désirée leapt from her chair. "Oh, good. Let me show you what the problem was. My brothers caution against…"

As soon as she and Redmire went out of the front door to inspect the newly repaired carriage, Jack took the dining chair opposite his children.

"I have a question." He rubbed the back of his neck. "I've asked you it before, and the answer was no, but I'd like to raise the topic again." He took a deep breath. "How would you feel if I… remarried?"

The twins exchanged glances. "Do we get to pick who?"

He tried not to smile. "Let me guess. Clever with '*remèdes*,' fearless with frogs, bearer of burnt-biscuit hair?"

They nodded.

"You can make her stay?" Frederick whispered.

Annie leaned forward. "Do you promise?"

"I can't make her do anything," Jack admitted.

It would not be an easy task. He wasn't just asking her to spend her life with him and his family. He'd be asking her to give up *her* family. Their dreams. Their shared future. Jack wouldn't blame her if her answer was to choose France.

Damn it. He shoved his fingers through his hair. It was a good thing he still hadn't responded to any of the governess queries.

He needed time to think of a plan.

CHAPTER 14

*A*fter morning lessons with the twins, Désirée exited the school room just in time to glimpse Jack stride toward the front door wearing riding attire.

"Where are you going?" she asked in surprise.

He made a face. "I completely forgot about a race I'd arranged with your brothers. Maybe a few mindless minutes with the wind in my hair will help revive my brain."

"I shall go with you," she said at once. "Two against one are horrid odds."

Her brothers raced carriages or horses almost every day of the year and had likely raced Jack a thousand other times without her hanging over their shoulders.

That was then. The situation had changed.

Lucien was becoming increasingly restless—and suspicious—of her extended "temporary" position in the Skeffington home, and likely planned to confront him with Bastien as his second.

If Jack showed up wearing an *I-just-despoiled-your-sister* expression, all hell would break loose.

He shrugged. "We're meeting on the track behind the Harpers' stud farm. Olive promised to loan me her fastest beast."

"Make that *two* fastest." Desiree grabbed her hat and a spencer. Riding clothes would be easier, but she didn't want to risk Jack going without her because she took too long.

They arrived at the farm in plenty of time to arrange for an extra horse. They were at the mouth of the lane leading through the evergreen forest in no time.

Her brothers were not yet present, but the sound of distant hoofbeats indicated they would arrive at any moment.

Before her brothers reached them, Jack spun in his saddle to face Désirée.

"I talked to my children," he blurted out. "We don't want you as interim governess."

"What?" she squeaked.

"You're so much more than a governess, and

'temporary' is no longer good enough. They want you as their mother and I want you as my wife."

"*What?*"

"I'm not asking you yet," he said quickly. "The answer is up to you, but I want to do this the right way. Starting with getting permission from your brothers first."

"W-what?"

But it was too late for private conversation. Her brothers were here.

Désirée's heart pounded. Jack wanted to *marry* her. He'd discussed it with his children, but he hadn't mentioned love or where he intended the family to live. She was not yet certain what her answer would be, but there was no question as to what her brothers would say:

Absolutely not.

"Désirée!" Their faces erupted into smiles at the sight of her, and they trotted their horses closer to kiss her cheeks.

"We're so glad you're here." Bastien grinned at her. "We've got some news."

Lucien leaned forward, unable to contain himself. "We have the money."

"What?" Désirée said faintly. She was starting to think that was the only word she had any use for anymore.

Lucien's eyes shone with excitement. "I said six months, did I not?"

"First you said a year," Bastien corrected him. "And then you said six months."

"And now I say tomorrow!" Lucien finished with glee.

"*What?*" This one came from Jack. At least Désirée wasn't the only one.

"We paid off the lease," Bastien explained.

"We could save up more money, but…" Lucien's hand made a gesture like brushing away flies. "Why wait?"

Jack looked like he'd swallowed a toad.

"I petitioned the government," Lucien continued with pride. "A few others have been successful at reclaiming some lands, so there is precedence for our request. However, we'll have to present ourselves in person for our case to be heard."

"Pack your valise," Bastien said, his eyes shining. "Can you believe we could have our old home back by Christmas? It'll be a dream come true."

Désirée touched her shaking chest as though she could keep her flailing heart inside. The thing was… it *would* be a dream come true.

She and her brothers had literally been dreaming of their return since the very day they left.

Her stomach twisted. She *wanted* her family's land to be restored to them. She wanted to sleep in her old bed, run barefoot through the old fields, smell flowers she hadn't even seen in eighteen long years.

She also wanted Jack. And Frederick. And Annie. If she could be in two places at once, she would do so in a heartbeat.

But her brothers needed her. They had taken care of her ever since she was too small to take care of herself, and now that she was grown, she could not abandon them or their dream.

If living all the way across town for five weeks had been hard, surviving in separate countries would be untenable. After all they'd been through together, she could not lose them now.

"Well?" Lucien prompted, eyes sparkling. "Are you ready to finally go home?"

Her throat hurt too much to allow words through, so she nodded stiffly instead.

The expression on Jack's face was neither hurt nor surprised, but doggedly stoic, as if he had never expected the two of them to ever truly live happily ever after.

She tried to meet his eyes, but he would not look her way. Her heart felt ripped asunder. At least it was better he have his answer without

asking the question, to save him the awkward-
ness of direct refusal.

He met her eyes at last.

"Family first," he said without inflection.

She nodded. He understood, even if he hated
her for it. *Family first* was his creed, too.

CHAPTER 15

*J*ack's heart beat far too fast. She was going to leave.

She was going to leave.

He could not say he was surprised. Nor could he object. She belonged in France, if that was what she wanted. She belonged with family.

But, if she wanted, she could also belong with him. With his family. It could be *their* family. If she wanted.

He had broken the subject badly. Lucien had presented a shining alternative before Jack could even present his case. *He* was the one who had provided the le Duc family the coin they needed to leave forever. He was *not* going to be the fool who let Désirée walk away for good without using his last chance to say what was in his heart.

Because he had said he would do so, Jack turned to Lucien first.

"Before anyone packs valises," Jack said softly. "I am officially asking permission to court your sister."

"To *marry* her?" Bastien's horse skittered backward.

Lucien's stallion did not move a muscle. "*No.*"

So much for the formalities. Jack threw pride to the wind. Let her brothers listen.

He turned to Désirée. "I should have told you how I feel long before this moment."

"I said no," Lucien snarled.

"She's twenty-seven and knows her own mind," Jack replied without taking his gaze off Désirée. "I asked your permission to be polite. Hers is the only opinion that matters."

She held her reins tight in her lap but did not speak.

He pushed on. "I love you."

Her expression of surprise indicated he had not made this factor nearly clear enough.

"I love you," he said again, louder this time. "I love your curiosity and your '*remèdes.*' I love how splendid you are with my children. I love your willingness to help everyone, be it broken axles or finding replacement governesses. I love how you trundle hoops and how you throw knives—"

"*What?*" Lucien interrupted.

"—and I love how you're always trying to make yourself better for everyone around you." He took in a breath. "But you don't have to. You're perfect just as you are. You don't need to practice French recipes to prove you're French. You *are* French."

"Of course she's French," Bastien muttered. "Nobody doubted she was French."

"—and you don't need to memorize English Christmas carols to prove you're English. You *are* English."

"She's definitely not English," Lucien said.

Désirée frowned. "You just said I was French."

"That's the magical part." He tried to make her see. "Nobody says you have to pick one."

"Literally everyone says that," Bastien put in.

Lucien nodded. "Whole wars have been fought over it."

"Bah." Jack waved a hand. "*Some* people might not be clever enough or open hearted enough to be the best of both places, but you aren't 'some people.' You're the sweetest, bravest, kindest, most off-key soprano I know." He gazed into her eyes. "I wouldn't want to spend my life with anyone else."

She stared back at him.

"I can't promise you forever," he said softly. "I learned the hard way that 'until death do we part' sometimes comes much sooner than expected. I grieved for years, too scared of another loss to risk putting my heart and my children through pain like that all over again. I wanted to shield them. To keep them safe. I was wrong."

Her brow furrowed. "Wrong?"

"Running away is the right answer when you're facing cannon fire or giant wasps. It's the wrong answer if you're running away from love. *You* are worth it. My children are worth it. *I* am worth it." He reached out his hand. "Marry me."

CHAPTER 16

*D*ésirée's heart fluttered too fast for her to catch a proper breath.

Before she could respond, Lucien muscled his horse forward. "She doesn't belong to you. She belongs with us. We are her real family. She is our blood." He turned his back without awaiting a reply. "Come, Désirée. We are leaving."

"No."

The lone syllable nearly unseated Lucien from his horse. "What did you say?"

"I said 'no.' I'm not finished here yet." She held her ground. "Jack is talking to *me* about *my* life. What I do with it needs to be my decision."

Bastien nudged his horse forward. "What do you want?"

Although those were the words he used, the

ones he meant were, *Who do you want?* Her chest grew tight.

How could she walk away from the man she loved?

How could she walk away from the family she loved?

Jack lived the life that she wanted. He had a home he belonged to, a family who adored him just as he was, an entire village that cherished him. The dangling carrot said *this could be yours, too* but the catch was having to turn her back on her own brothers to accept it.

Lucien and Sébastien had been just as terrified and grief-stricken as she was when they'd been forced from their home... but they hadn't let her know. They told her everything was going to be fine. That they would always protect her. That no one would ever again have the power to separate their family.

All three of them had vowed to do anything it took to one day make it home.

Her whole life, Désirée had avoided hard choices by always siding with whatever her family wanted to do. By choosing unity over division. By choosing the group over herself.

Now, no matter which path she took, she would be choosing someone she loved over someone else she loved. The road had divided. She might be equal parts English and French, but she could not be in France and England at the same time.

Her brothers wanted the best for her. They always had and always would. They'd dedicated their lives to find a way to retrieve everything they felt she was owed. Status. A dowry. An aristocratic French husband.

Jack didn't want anything from her. He didn't need her dowry. He had his own land, his own money. He did not care about her status or want to change her in any way.

He just wanted to love her. Maybe not forever, but for as long as they could.

She gathered her reins with trembling fingers and turned to face her brothers.

"We did not choose to be siblings, but no sister could ask for better ones. I love you both to the heavens and back. I always have and always will."

They exchanged relieved glances.

She sucked in a shaky breath. "But I cannot be something I am not, just because it is what you command. You seek 'what's best for me' but do not ask what *I* want, what *I* would like best. I do not wish to divide our families. I wish to forge an even bigger one."

Jack's startled gaze met hers.

Désirée straightened her shoulders. "My family is Lucien. My family is Bastien. My family is Jack and Frederick and Annie. They demand nothing from me, but ask if I might carve out a space for them in my heart. I have already done so, willingly and happily. There is no need to ask. Jack, I love you, too. All three of you."

His lips parted.

She was not yet done. She turned to Lucien. "I will go to France and present myself to the court with my brothers. But I will not stay, unless all of us stay. If Jack and the children wish to remain here in Cressmouth, in the home that they have made into my home too, then that is where I belong." She held out her hand to Jack. "Here. With you."

He did not take her hand in his. "I couldn't forgive myself if marriage to me ruined your bond with your brothers."

"Only a man who deserved her would say so," Lucien said gruffly. "My perspective has not changed. Family always comes first. And now that I know this man and his children are your family..." He inclined his head to Jack. "Then they are my family, too."

"You've just been given permission," Bastien whispered. "Run off with my sister before he changes his mind."

Désirée entwined her fingers with Jack's, and they did exactly that.

CHAPTER 17

Three weeks later

*J*ack and Désirée stood before the
vicar in the castle chapel. Although
most weddings were private affairs,
more villagers and neighbors crowded around
them than could fit in the pews. Possibly because they'd heard the wedding breakfast would
also feature Jack's infamous wassail.

Frederick and Annie were in the first row,
between Bastien and Lucien. Although the
chapel hummed with low murmurs whilst the
minister prepared his notes, the twins' loud
whispers stood out from the rest.

"Legendary." Annie gazed at the crowd with

satisfaction. "Everyone has come to watch the duke's bride be wed."

"Stop trying to make Papa a Christmas duke," Frederick hissed. "He is not a duke. Désirée is the duke!"

Annie sniffed. "Then *he* is the duke's bride."

Frederick looked as though he might throttle his sister. "Papa can't be a bride. He's a groom."

"Then Désirée is…" Annie's face wrinkled in consternation. "A duke-bride?"

"Very well. Yes. She is 'le Duc bride.'" Frederick pinched Annie's leg. "Now, be quiet and watch. They're starting."

Unable to stop himself, Jack grinned at the loveliest duke-bride in England.

Your Grace, she mouthed back to him, and winked.

At last, the minister addressed them. "The vows you are about to take are to be made in the presence of God, who is judge of all and knows all the secrets of our hearts."

Jack nodded. It didn't matter whether he was all alone or judged by the entire world. The woman standing across from him was the keeper of his heart.

"Jack Skeffington," the minister continued. "Will you take Désirée le Duc to be your wife? Will you love her, comfort her, honor and protect her, and, forsaking all others, be faithful to her as long as you both shall live?"

He squeezed her hands. "For as long as my heart still beats and there is breath in my chest. I will."

"Désirée le Duc." The vicar turned to face her. "Will you take Jack Skeffington to be your husband? Will you love him, comfort him, honor and protect him, and, forsaking all others, be faithful to him as long as you both shall live?"

She smiled up at him. "For as long as the world has wine to drink and carols to sing. I will."

And so it was.

EPILOGUE

Six years later
Margaux, France

"*A*re you scared?" Frederick asked Annie.

"Of a come-out? Hardly." She tucked a flower behind her ear. "Sixteen is grown up. We've been going to Cressmouth assemblies for years. How much different can London be?"

"You were scared when we first came to France," he reminded her.

"*You* were scared," she shot back. "Even though Papa told you we'd only spend summers here, and winters back home."

"I was disadvantaged!" he protested. "You

started French lessons two years earlier and didn't even tell me!"

She flashed him an innocent smile. *"Je suis désolée. La vie est pleine de joies et de déceptions."*

"Enfants," Désirée called. "Might you stop bickering long enough to celebrate our vineyard's first harvest?"

They raced over to the soft yellow blanket spread across the rolling green grass. Jack knelt in the center, holding aloft a freshly uncorked bottle of wine as if it were a prize given to him by the heavens.

He poured each of them a glass, then lifted his own. "To France!"

Désirée raised her wine. "To England."

Frederick lifted his in toast. "To the Skeffington vineyard's prosperous future."

"And above all..." Annie's eyes twinkled mischievously as she raised her glass. "To rakes who steal kisses."

"Annie!" Jack and Frederick scolded in unison.

Désirée and Annie drank their wine and collapsed against each other in giggles.

"I don't know why you're laughing," Jack grumbled to Désirée. "As I recall, you stole the first kiss."

She grinned back at him. "In that case, I'd say it was my most successful *'remède'* of all."

THE END

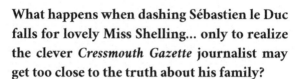

What happens when dashing Sébastien le Duc falls for lovely Miss Shelling... only to realize the clever *Cressmouth Gazette* journalist may get too close to the truth about his family?

Join the fun in *The Duke's Embrace*, the next romance in the *12 Dukes of Christmas* series!

ACKNOWLEDGMENTS

As always, I could not have written this book without the invaluable support of my critique partner, beta readers, and editors. Huge thanks go out to Erica Monroe and Tessa Shapcott. You are the best!

Lastly, I want to thank the *12 Dukes of Christmas* facebook group, my *Historical Romance Book Club*, and my fabulous street team. Your enthusiasm makes the romance happen.

Thank you so much!

THANK YOU FOR READING

Love talking books with fellow readers?

Join the *Historical Romance Book Club* for prizes, books, and live chats with your favorite romance authors:
Facebook.com/groups/HistRomBookClub

Check out the *12 Dukes of Christmas* facebook group for giveaways and exclusive content:
Facebook.com/groups/DukesOfChristmas

Join the *Rogues to Riches* facebook group for insider info and first looks at future books in the series:
Facebook.com/groups/RoguesToRiches

Check out the *Dukes of War* facebook group for giveaways and exclusive content:

Facebook.com/groups/DukesOfWar

And check out the official website for sneak peeks and more:

www.EricaRidley.com/books

THE DUKE'S EMBRACE

Unpaid and under-appreciated journalist Miss Eve Shelling never goes anywhere without a trusty notebook and her overprotective Duenna —who happens to be a bullmastiff. Eve learned the hard way that men are not to be trusted. She's definitely not falling head-over-heels for the deceptively charming subject of her front-page column.

Local blacksmith Monsieur Sébastien le Duc is the pillar of his community—when he's not pillaging elsewhere. He's a rakish dandy with a heart of stolen gold and two teeny tiny secrets. One happens to be a wee international smuggling operation. The other involves losing his heart to an ambitious journalist determined to expose the truth at any cost...

The *12 Dukes of Christmas* is a series of heart-warming Regency romps nestled in a picturesque snow-covered village. Twelve delightful romances... and plenty of delicious dukes!

ABOUT THE AUTHOR

Erica Ridley is a *New York Times* and *USA Today* best-selling author of historical romance novels.

In the new *12 Dukes of Christmas* series, enjoy witty, heartwarming Regency romps nestled in a picturesque snow-covered village. After all, nothing heats up a winter night quite like finding oneself in the arms of a duke!

Her two most popular series, the *Dukes of War* and *Rogues to Riches*, feature roguish peers and dashing war heroes who find love amongst the splendor and madness of Regency England.

When not reading or writing romances, Erica can be found riding camels in Africa, zip-lining through rainforests in Central America, or getting hopelessly lost in the middle of Budapest.

∾

Let's be friends! Find Erica on:
www.EricaRidley.com

Made in the USA
Monee, IL
12 December 2022

21164228R00121